Marx
Joyce
Defoe Abbott Hardy Machiavelli Chesterton Emerson Austen
Melville Montaigne Cooper Haggard Hugo Grimm
Stoker Carroll Christie Molière Eliot
Wilde Maupassant Byron Schiller
Garnett Fitzgerald Engels Smith Kafka
Goethe Einstein Hawthorne Hall
Cotton Dostoyevsky Willis
Baum Henry Kipling Doyle
Leslie Dumas Flaubert Turgenev Nietzsche Balzac Crane
Stockton Vatsyayana Verne
Burroughs Whitman Gogol Vinci
Curtis Tocqueville Busch
Homer Widger Tolstoy
Darwin Thoreau Twain Scott
Potter Freud Zola Plato Harte
Kant Jowett Lawrence Dickens Hesse
Stevenson Burton
Andersen Cervantes
London Descartes Voltaire
Poe Aristotle Wells Cooke
Hale James Hastings
Bunner Shakespeare Irving
Richter Chambers
Doré da Shaw Benedict Alcott
Dante Chekhov Pushkin
Swift Wodehouse Newton

Amabel Channice

Anne Douglas Sedgwick

Imprint

This book is part of TREDITION CLASSICS

Author: Anne Douglas Sedgwick
Cover design: Buchgut, Berlin – Germany

Publisher: tredition GmbH, Hamburg - Germany
ISBN: 978-3-8472-1589-9

www.tredition.com
www.tredition.de

AMABEL CHANNICE

ANNE DOUGLAS SEDGWICK

Amabel Channice

BY

Anne Douglas Sedgwick

AUTHOR OF "THE RESCUE," "PATHS OF JUDGEMENT," "A FOUNTAIN SEALED," ETC.

NEW YORK
The Century Co.
1908

AMABEL CHANNICE

I

L ady Channice was waiting for her son to come in from the garden. The afternoon was growing late, but she had not sat down to the table, though tea was ready and the kettle sent out a narrow banner of steam. Walking up and down the long room she paused now and then to look at the bowls and vases of roses placed about it, now and then to look out of the windows, and finally at the last window she stopped to watch Augustine advancing over the lawn towards the house. It was a grey stone house, low and solid, its bareness unalleviated by any grace of ornament or structure, and its two long rows of windows gazed out resignedly at a tame prospect. The stretch of lawn sloped to a sunken stone wall; beyond the wall a stream ran sluggishly in a ditch-like channel; on the left the grounds were shut in by a sycamore wood, and beyond were flat meadows crossed in the distance by lines of tree-bordered roads. It was a peaceful, if not a cheering prospect. Lady Channice was fond of it. Cheerfulness was not a thing she looked for; but she looked for peace, and it was peace she found in the flat green distance, the far, reticent ripple of hill on the horizon, the dark forms of the sycamores. Her only regret for the view was that it should miss the sunrise and sunset; in the evenings, beyond the silhouetted woods, one saw the golden sky; but the house faced north, and it was for this that the green of the lawn was so dank, and the grey of the walls so cold, and the light in the drawing-room where Lady Channice stood so white and so monotonous.

She was fond of the drawing-room, also, unbeautiful and grave to sadness though it was. The walls were wainscotted to the ceiling with ancient oak, so that though the north light entered at four high windows the room seemed dark. The furniture was ugly, miscellaneous and inappropriate. The room had been dismantled, and in place of the former drawing-room suite were gathered together incongruous waifs and strays from dining- and smoking-room and boudoir. A number of heavy chairs predominated covered in a maroon leather which had cracked in places; and there were three lugubrious sofas to match.

By degrees, during her long and lonely years at Charlock House, Lady Channice had, at first tentatively, then with a growing assurance in her limited sphere of action, moved away all the ugliest, most trivial things: tattered brocade and gilt footstools, faded antimacassars, dismal groups of birds and butterflies under glass cases. When she sat alone in the evening, after Augustine, as child or boy, had gone to bed, the ghostly glimmer of the birds, the furtive glitter of a glass eye here and there, had seemed to her quite dreadful. The removal of the cases (they were large and heavy, and Mrs. Bray, the housekeeper, had looked grimly disapproving)—was her crowning act of courage, and ever since their departure she had breathed more freely. It had been easier to dispose of all the little colonies of faded photographs that stood on cabinets and tables; they were photographs of her husband's family and of his family's friends, people most of whom were quite unknown to her, and their continued presence in the abandoned house was due to indifference, not affection: no one had cared enough about them to put them away, far less to look at them. After looking at them for some years,— these girls in court dress of a bygone fashion, huntsmen holding crops, sashed babies and matrons in caps or tiaras,—Lady Channice had cared enough to put them away. She had not, either, to ask for Mrs. Bray's assistance or advice for this, a fact which was a relief, for Mrs. Bray was a rather dismal being and reminded her, indeed, of the stuffed birds in the removed glass cases. With her own hands she incarcerated the photographs in the drawers of a heavily carved bureau and turned the keys upon them.

The only ornaments now, were the pale roses, the books, and, above her writing-desk, a little picture that she had brought with her, a water-colour sketch of her old home painted by her mother many years ago.

So the room looked very bare. It almost looked like the parlour of a convent; with a little more austerity, whitened walls and a few thick velvet and gilt lives of the saints on the tables, the likeness would have been complete. The house itself was conventual in aspect, and Lady Channice, as she stood there in the quiet light at the window, looked not unlike a nun, were it not for her crown of pale gold hair that shone in the dark room and seemed, like the roses, to bring into it the brightness of an outer, happier world.

She was a tall woman of forty, her ample form, her wide bosom, the falling folds of her black dress, her loosely girdled waist, suggesting, with the cloistral analogies, the mournful benignity of a bereaved Madonna. Seen as she stood there, leaning her head to watch her son's approach, she was an almost intimidating presence, black, still, and stately. But when the door opened and the young man came in, when, not moving to meet him, she turned her head with a slight smile of welcome, all intimidating impressions passed away. Her face, rather, as it turned, under its crown of gold, was the intimidated face. It was curiously young, pure, flawless, as though its youth and innocence had been preserved in some crystal medium of prayer and silence; and if the nun-like analogies failed in their awe-inspiring associations, they remained in the associations of unconscious pathos and unconscious appeal. Amabel Channice's face, like her form, was long and delicately ample; its pallor that of a flower grown in shadow; the mask a little over-large for the features. Her eyes were small, beautifully shaped, slightly slanting upwards, their light grey darkened under golden lashes, the brows definitely though palely marked. Her mouth was pale coral-colour, and the small upper lip, lifting when she smiled as she was smiling now, showed teeth of an infantile, milky whiteness. The smile was charming, timid, tentative, ingratiating, like a young girl's, and her eyes were timid, too, and a little wild.

"Have you had a good read?" she asked her son. He had a book in his hand.

"Very, thanks. But it is getting chilly, down there in the meadow. And what a lot of frogs there are in the ditch," said Augustine smiling, "they were jumping all over the place."

"Oh, as long as they weren't toads!" said Lady Channice, her smile lighting in response. "When I came here first to live there were so many toads, in the stone areas, you know, under the gratings in front of the cellar windows. You can't imagine how many! It used quite to terrify me to look at them and I went to the front of the house as seldom as possible. I had them all taken away, finally, in baskets,—not killed, you know, poor things,—but just taken and put down in a field a mile off. I hope they didn't starve;—but toads are very intelligent, aren't they; one always associates them with fairy-tales and princes."

She had gone to the tea-table while she spoke and was pouring the boiling water into the teapot. Her voice had pretty, flute-like ups and downs in it and a questioning, upward cadence at the end of sentences. Her upper lip, her smile, the run of her speech, all would have made one think her humorous, were it not for the strain of nervousness that one felt in her very volubility.

Her son lent her a kindly but rather vague attention while she talked to him about the toads, and his eye as he stood watching her make the tea was also vague. He sat down presently, as if suddenly remembering why he had come in, and it was only after a little interval of silence, in which he took his cup from his mother's hands, that something else seemed to occur to him as suddenly, a late arriving suggestion from her speech.

"What a horribly gloomy place you must have found it."

Her eyes, turning on him quickly, lost, in an instant, their uncertain gaiety.

"Gloomy? Is it gloomy? Do you feel it gloomy here, Augustine?"

"Oh, well, no, not exactly," he answered easily. "You see I've always been used to it. You weren't."

As she said nothing to this, seeming at a loss for any reply, he went on presently to talk of other things, of the book he had been reading, a heavy metaphysical tome; of books that he intended to read; of a letter that he had received that morning from the Eton friend with whom he was going up to Oxford for his first term. His mother listened, showing a careful interest usual with her, but after another little silence she said suddenly:

"I think it's a very nice place, Charlock House, Augustine. Your father wouldn't have wanted me to live here if he'd imagined that I could find it gloomy, you know."

"Oh, of course not," said the young man, in an impassive, pleasant voice.

"He has always, in everything, been so thoughtful for my comfort and happiness," said Lady Channice.

Augustine did not look at her: his eyes were fixed on the sky outside and he seemed to be reflecting—though not over her words.

"So that I couldn't bear him ever to hear anything of that sort," Lady Channice went on, "that either of us could find it gloomy, I mean. You wouldn't ever say it to him, would you, Augustine." There was a note at once of urgency and appeal in her voice.

"Of course not, since you don't wish it," her son replied.

"I ask you just because it happens that your father is coming," Lady Channice said, "tomorrow;—and, you see, if you had this in your mind, you might have said something. He is coming to spend the afternoon."

He looked at her now, steadily, still pleasantly; but his colour rose.

"Really," he said.

"Isn't it nice. I do hope that it will be fine; these Autumn days are so uncertain; if only the weather holds up we can have a walk perhaps."

"Oh, I think it will hold up. Will there be time for a walk?"

"He will be here soon after lunch, and, I think, stay on to tea."

"He didn't stay on to tea the last time, did he."

"No, not last time; he is so very busy; it's quite three years since we have had that nice walk over the meadows, and he likes that so much."

She was trying to speak lightly and easily. "And it must be quite a year since you have seen him."

"Quite," said Augustine. "I never see him, hardly, but here, you know."

He was still making his attempt at pleasantness, but something hard and strained had come into his voice, and as, with a sort of helplessness, her resources exhausted, his mother sat silent, he went on, glancing at her, as if with the sudden resolution, he also wanted to make very sure of his way;—

"You like seeing him more than anything, don't you; though you are separated."

Augustine Channice talked a great deal to his mother about outside things, such as philosophy; but of personal things, of their relation to the world, to each other, to his father, he never spoke. So that his speaking now was arresting.

His mother gazed at him. "Separated? We have always been the best of friends."

"Of course. I mean—that you've never cared to live together.—Incompatibility, I suppose. Only," Augustine did not smile, he looked steadily at his mother, "I should think that since you are so fond of him you'd like seeing him oftener. I should think that since he is the best of friends he would want to come oftener, you know."

When he had said these words he flushed violently. It was an echo of his mother's flush. And she sat silent, finding no words.

"Mother," said Augustine, "forgive me. That was impertinent of me. It's no affair of mine."

She thought so, too, apparently, for she found no words in which to tell him that it was his affair. Her hands clasped tightly in her lap, her eyes downcast, she seemed shrunken together, overcome by his tactless intrusion.

"Forgive me," Augustine repeated.

The supplication brought her the resource of words again. "Of course, dear. It is only—I can't explain it to you. It is very complicated. But, though it seems so strange to you,—to everybody, I know—it is just that: though we don't live together, and though I see so little of your father, I do care for him very, very much. More than for anybody in the world,—except you, of course, dear Augustine."

"Oh, don't be polite to me," he said, and smiled. "More than for anybody in the world; stick to it."

She could but accept the amendment, so kindly and, apparently, so lightly pressed upon her, and she answered him with a faint, a grateful smile, saying, in a low voice:—"You see, dear, he is the noblest person I have ever known." Tears were in her eyes. Augustine turned away his own.

They sat then for a little while in silence, the mother and son.

Her eyes downcast, her hands folded in an attitude that suggested some inner dedication, Amabel Channice seemed to stay her thoughts on the vision of that nobility. And though her son was near her, the thoughts were far from him.

It was characteristic of Augustine Channice, when he mused, to gaze straight before him, whatever the object might be that met his unseeing eyes. The object now was the high Autumnal sky outside, crossed only here and there by a drifting fleet of clouds.

The light fell calmly upon the mother and son and, in their stillness, their contemplation, the two faces were like those on an old canvas, preserved from time and change in the trance-like immutability of art. In colour, the two heads chimed, though Augustine's hair was vehemently gold and there were under-tones of brown and amber in his skin. But the oval of Lady Channice's face grew angular in her son's, broader and more defiant; so that, palely, darkly white and gold, on their deep background, the two heads emphasized each other's character by contrast. Augustine's lips were square and scornful; his nose ruggedly bridged; his eyes, under broad eyebrows, ringed round the iris with a line of vivid hazel; and as his lips, though mild in expression, were scornful in form, so these eyes, even in their contemplation, seemed fierce. Calm, controlled face as it was, its meaning for the spectator was of something passionate and implacable. In mother and son alike one felt a capacity for endurance almost tragic; but while Augustine's would be the endurance of the rock, to be moved only by shattering, his mother's was the endurance of the flower, that bends before the tempest, unresisting, beaten down into the earth, but lying, even there, unbroken.

II

T he noise and movement of an outer world seemed to break in upon the recorded vision of arrested life.

The door opened, a quick, decisive step approached down the hall, and, closely following the announcing maid, Mrs. Grey, the local squiress, entered the room. In the normal run of rural conventions, Lady Channice should have held the place; but Charlock House no longer stood for what it had used to stand in the days of Sir Hugh Channice's forbears. Mrs. Grey, of Pangley Hall, had never held any but the first place and a consciousness of this fact seemed to radiate from her competent personality. She was a vast middle-aged woman clad in tweed and leather, but her abundance of firm, hard flesh could lend itself to the roughest exigences of a sporting outdoor life. Her broad face shone like a ripe apple, and her sharp eyes, her tight lips, the cheerful creases of her face, expressed an observant and rather tyrannous good-temper.

"Tea? No, thanks; no tea for me," she almost shouted; "I've just had tea with Mrs. Grier. How are you, Lady Channice? and you, Augustine? What a man you are getting to be; a good inch taller than my Tom. Reading as usual, I see. I can't get my boys to look at a book in vacation time. What's the book? Ah, fuddling your brains with that stuff, still, are you? Still determined to be a philosopher? Do you really want him to be a philosopher, my dear?"

"Indeed I think it would be very nice if he could be a philosopher," said Lady Channice, smiling, for though she had often to evade Mrs. Grey's tyranny she liked her good temper. She seemed in her reply to float, lightly and almost gaily above Mrs. Grey, and away from her. Mrs. Grey was accustomed to these tactics and it was characteristic of her not to let people float away if she could possibly help it. This matter of Augustine's future was frequently in dispute between them. Her feet planted firmly, her rifle at her shoulder, she seemed now to take aim at a bird that flew from her.

"And of course you encourage him! You read with him and study with him! And you won't see that you let him drift more and more out of practical life and into moonshine. What does it do for him, that's what I ask? Where does it lead him? What's the good of it? Why he'll finish as a fusty old don. Does it make you a better man, Augustine, or a happier one, to spend all your time reading philosophy?"

"Very much better, very much happier, I find:—but I don't give it all my time, you know," Augustine answered, with much his mother's manner of light evasion. He let Mrs. Grey see that he found her funny; perhaps he wished to let her see that philosophy helped him to. Mrs. Grey gave up the fantastic bird and turned on her heel.

"Well, I've not come to dispute, as usual, with you, Augustine. I've come to ask you, Lady Channice, if you won't, for once, break through your rules and come to tea on Sunday. I've a surprise for you. An old friend of yours is to be of our party for this week-end. Lady Elliston; she comes tomorrow, and she writes that she hopes to see something of you."

Mrs. Grey had her eye rather sharply on Lady Channice; she expected to see her colour rise, and it did rise.

"Lady Elliston?" she repeated, vaguely, or, perhaps, faintly.

"Yes; you did know her; well, she told me."

"It was years ago," said Lady Channice, looking down; "Yes, I knew her quite well. It would be very nice to see her again. But I don't think I will break my rule; thank you so much."

Mrs. Grey looked a little disconcerted and a little displeased. "Now that you are growing up, Augustine," she said, "you must shake your mother out of her way of life. It's bad for her. She lives here, quite alone, and, when you are away—as you will have to be more and more, for some time now,—she sees nobody but her village girls, Mrs. Grier and me from one month's end to the other. I can't think what she's made of. I should go mad. And so many of us would be delighted if she would drop in to tea with us now and then."

"Oh, well, you can drop in to tea with her instead," said Augustine. His mother sat silent, with her faint smile.

"Well, I do. But I'm not enough, though I flatter myself that I'm a good deal. It's unwholesome, such a life, downright morbid and unwholesome. One should mingle with one's kind. I shall wonder at you, Augustine, if you allow it, just as, for years, I've wondered at your father."

It may have been her own slight confusion, or it may have been something exasperating in Lady Channice's silence, that had precipitated Mrs. Grey upon this speech, but, when she had made it, she became very red and wondered whether she had gone too far. Mrs. Grey was prepared to go far. If people evaded her, and showed an unwillingness to let her be kind to them—on her own terms,—terms which, in regard to Lady Channice, were very strictly defined;—if people would behave in this unbecoming and ungrateful fashion, they only got, so Mrs. Grey would have put it, what they jolly well deserved if she gave them a "stinger." But Mrs. Grey did not like to give Lady Channice "stingers"; therefore she now became red and wondered at herself.

Lady Channice had lifted her eyes and it was as if Mrs. Grey saw walls and moats and impenetrable thickets glooming in them. She answered for Augustine: "My husband and I have always been in perfect agreement on the matter."

Mrs. Grey tried a cheerful laugh;—"You won him over, too, no doubt."

"Entirely."

"Well, Augustine," Mrs. Grey turned to the young man again, "I don't succeed with your mother, but I hope for better luck with you. You're a man, now, and not yet, at all events, a monk. Won't you dine with us on Saturday night?"

Now Mrs. Grey was kind; but she had never asked Lady Channice to dinner. The line had been drawn, firmly drawn years ago— and by Mrs. Grey herself—at tea. And it was not until Lady Channice had lived for several years at Charlock House, when it became evident that, in spite of all that was suspicious, not to say sinister, in her situation, she was not exactly cast off and that her husband, so to speak, admitted her to tea if not to dinner,—it was not until then that Mrs. Grey voiced at once the tolerance and the discretion of the neighbourhood and said: "They are on friendly terms; he comes to see her twice a year. We can call; she need not be asked to anything but tea. There can be no harm in that."

There was, indeed, no harm, for though, when they did call in Mrs. Grey's broad wake, they were received with gentle courtesy, they were made to feel that social contacts would go no further. Lady Channice had been either too much offended or too much frightened by the years of ostracism, or perhaps it was really by her own choice that she adopted the attitude of a person who saw people when they came to her but who never went to see them. This attitude, accepted by the few, was resented by the many, so that hardly anybody ever called upon Lady Channice. And so it was that Mrs. Grey satisfied at once benevolence and curiosity in her staunch visits to the recluse of Charlock House, and could feel herself as Lady Channice's one wholesome link with the world that she had rejected or—here lay all the ambiguity, all the mystery that, for years, had whetted Mrs. Grey's curiosity to fever-point—that had rejected her.

As Augustine grew up the situation became more complicated. It was felt that as the future owner of Charlock House and inheritor of his mother's fortune Augustine was not to be tentatively taken up but decisively seized. People had resented Sir Hugh's indifference to Charlock House, the fact that he had never lived there and had tried, just before his marriage, to sell it. But Augustine was yet blameless, and Augustine would one day be a wealthy not an impecunious squire, and Mrs. Grey had said that she would see to it that Augustine had his chance. "Apparently there's no one to bring him out, unless I do," she said. "His father, it seems, won't, and his mother can't. One doesn't know what to think, or, at all events, one keeps what one thinks to oneself, for she is a good, sweet creature, whatever her faults may have been. But Augustine shall be asked to dinner one day."

Augustine's "chance," in Mrs. Grey's eye, was her sixth daughter, Marjory.

So now the first step up the ladder was being given to Augustine.

He kept his vagueness, his lightness, his coolly pleasant smile, looking at Mrs. Grey and not at his mother as he answered: "Thanks so much, but I'm monastic, too, you know. I don't go to dinners. I'll ride over some afternoon and see you all."

Mrs. Grey compressed her lips. She was hurt and she had, also, some difficulty in restraining her temper before this rebuff. "But you go to dinners in London. You stay with people."

"Ah, yes; but I'm alone then. When I'm with my mother I share her life." He spoke so lightly, yet so decisively, with a tact and firmness beyond his years, that Mrs. Grey rose, accepting her defeat.

"Then Lady Elliston and I will come over, some day," she said. "I wish we saw more of her. John and I met her while we were staying with the Bishop this Spring. The Bishop has the highest opinion of her. He said that she was a most unusual woman,—in the world, yet not of it. One feels that. Her eldest girl married young Lord Catesby, you know; a very brilliant match; she presents her second girl next Spring, when I do Marjory. You must come over for a ride with Marjory, soon, Augustine."

"I will, very soon," said Augustine.

When their visitor at last went, when the tramp of her heavy boots had receded down the hall, Lady Channice and her son again sat in silence; but it was now another silence from that into which Mrs. Grey's shots had broken. It was like the stillness of the copse or hedgerow when the sportsmen are gone and a vague stir and rustle in ditch or underbrush tells of broken wings or limbs, of a wounded thing hiding.

Lady Channice spoke at last. "I wish you had accepted for the dinner, Augustine. I don't want you to identify yourself with my peculiarities."

"I didn't want to dine with Mrs. Grey, mother."

"You hurt her. She is a kind neighbour. You will see her more or less for all of your life, probably. You must take your place, here, Augustine."

"My place is taken. I like it just as it is. I'll see the Greys as I always have seen them; I'll go over to tea now and then and I'll ride and hunt with the children."

"But that was when you were a child. You are almost a man now; you are a man, Augustine; and your place isn't a child's place."

"My place is by you." For the second time that day there was a new note in Augustine's voice. It was as if, clearly and definitely, for the first time, he was feeling something and seeing something and as if, though very resolutely keeping from her what he felt, he was, when pushed to it, as resolutely determined to let her see what he saw.

"By me, dear," she said faintly. "What do you mean?"

"She ought to have asked you to dinner, too."

"But I would not have accepted; I don't go out. She knows that. She knows that I am a real recluse."

"She ought to have asked knowing that you would not accept."

"Augustine dear, you are foolish. You know nothing of these little feminine social compacts."

"Are they only feminine?"

"Only. Mere crystallised conveniences. It would be absurd for Mrs. Grey, after all these years, to ask me in order to be refused."

There was a moment's silence and then Augustine said: "Did she ever ask you?"

The candles had been lighted and the lamp brought in, making the corners of the room look darker. There was only a vague radiance about the chimney piece, the little candle-flames doubled in the mirror, and the bright circle where Lady Channice and her son sat on either side of the large, round table. The lamp had a green shade, and their faces were in shadow. Augustine had turned away his eyes.

And now a strange and painful thing happened, stranger and more painful than he could have foreseen; for his mother did not answer him. The silence grew long and she did not speak. Augustine looked at her at last and saw that she was gazing at him, and, it seemed to him, with helpless fear. His own eyes did not echo it; anger, rather, rose in them, cold fierceness, against himself, it was apparent, as well as against the world that he suspected. He was not impulsive; he was not demonstrative; but he got up and put his hand on her shoulder. "I don't mean to torment you, like the rest of them," he said. "I don't mean to ask—and be refused. Forget what I said. It's only—only—that it infuriates me.—To see them all.—And you!—cut off, wasted, in prison here. I've been seeing it for a long time; I won't speak of it again. I know that there are sad things in your life. All I want to say, all I wanted to say was—that I'm with you, and against them."

She sat, her face in shadow beneath him, her hands tightly clasped together and pressed down upon her lap. And, in a faltering voice that strove in vain for firmness, she said: "Dear Augustine—thank you. I know you wouldn't want to hurt me. You see, when I came here to live, I had parted—from your father, and I wanted to be quite alone; I wanted to see no one. And they felt that: they felt that I wouldn't lead the usual life. So it grew most naturally. Don't be angry with people, or with the world. That would warp you, from the beginning. It's a good world, Augustine. I've found it so. It is sad, but there is such beauty.—I'm not cut off, or wasted;—I'm not in prison.—How can you say it, dear, of me, who have you—and *him*."

Augustine's hand rested on her shoulder for some moments more. Lifting it he stood looking before him. "I'm not going to quarrel with the world," he then said. "I know what I like in it."

"Dear—thanks—" she murmured.

Augustine picked up his book again. "I'll study for a bit, now, in my room," he said. "Will you rest before dinner? Do; I shall feel more easy in my conscience if I inflict Hegel on you afterwards."

III

L ady Channice did not go and rest. She sat on in the shadowy room gazing before her, her hands still clasped, her face wearing still its look of fear. For twenty years she had not known what it was to be without fear. It had become as much a part of her life as the air she breathed and any peace or gladness had blossomed for her only in that air: sometimes she was almost unconscious of it. This afternoon she had become conscious. It was as if the air were heavy and oppressive and as if she breathed with difficulty. And sitting there she asked herself if the time was coming when she must tell Augustine.

What she might have to tell was a story that seemed strangely disproportionate: it was the story of her life; but all of it that mattered, all of it that made the story, was pressed into one year long ago. Before that year was sunny, uneventful girlhood, after it grey, uneventful womanhood; the incident, the drama, was all knotted into one year, and it seemed to belong to herself no longer; she seemed a spectator, looking back in wonder at the disaster of another woman's life. A long flat road stretched out behind her; she had journeyed over it for years; and on the far horizon she saw, if she looked back, the smoke and flames of a burning city—miles and miles away.

Amabel Freer was the daughter of a rural Dean, a scholarly, sceptical man. The forms of religion were his without its heart; its heart was her mother's, who was saintly and whose orthodoxy was the vaguest symbolic system. From her father Amabel had the scholar's love of beauty in thought, from her mother the love of beauty in life; but her loves had been dreamy: she had thought and lived little. Happy compliance, happy confidence, a dawn-like sense of sweetness and purity, had filled her girlhood.

When she was sixteen her father had died, and her mother in the following year. Amabel and her brother Bertram were well dowered. Bertram was in the Foreign Office, neither saintly nor scholarly, like his parents, nor undeveloped like his young sister. He was a capable, conventional man of the world, sure of himself and rather suspicious of others. Amabel imagined him a model of all that was good and lovely. The sudden bereavement of her youth bewildered and overwhelmed her; her capacity for dependent, self-devoting love sought for an object and lavished itself upon her brother. She went to live with an aunt, her father's sister, and when she was eighteen her aunt brought her to London, a tall, heavy and rather clumsy country girl, arrested rather than developed by grief. Her aunt was a world-worn, harassed woman; she had married off her four daughters with difficulty and felt the need of a change of occupation; but she accepted as a matter of course the duty of marrying off Amabel. That task accomplished she would go to bed every night at half past ten and devote her days to collecting coins and enamels. Her respite came far more quickly than she could have imagined possible. Amabel had promise of great beauty, but two or three years were needed to fulfill it; Mrs. Compton could but be surprised when Sir Hugh Channice, an older colleague of Bertram's, a fashionable and charming man, asked for the hand of her unformed young charge. Sir Hugh was fourteen years Amabel's senior and her very guilelessness no doubt attracted him; then there was the money; he was not well off and he lived a life rather hazardously full. Still, Mrs. Compton could hardly believe in her good-fortune. Amabel accepted her own very simply; her compliance and confidence were even deeper than before. Sir Hugh was the most graceful of lovers. His quizzical tenderness reminded her of her father, his quasi-paternal courtship emphasized her instinctive trust in the beauty and goodness of life.

So at eighteen she was married at St. George's Hanover Square and wore a wonderful long satin train and her mothers lace veil and her mother's pearls around her neck and hair. A bridesmaid had said that pearls were unlucky, but Mrs. Compton tersely an-swered:—"Not if they are such good ones as these." Amabel had bowed her head to the pearls, seeing them, with the train, and the veil, and her own snowy figure, vaguely, still in the dreamlike haze. Memories of her father and mother, and of the dear deanery among its meadows, floating fragments of the poetry her father had loved, of the prayers her mother had taught her in childhood, hovered in her mind. She seemed to see the primrose woods where she had wandered, and to hear the sound of brooks and birds in Spring. A vague smile was on her lips. She thought of Sir Hugh as of a radi-ance lighting all. She was the happiest of girls.

Shortly after her marriage, all the radiance, all the haze was gone. It had been difficult then to know why. Now, as she looked back, she thought that she could understand.

She had been curiously young, curiously inexperienced. She had expected life to go on as dawn for ever. Everyday light had filled her with bleakness and disillusion. She had had childish fancies; that her husband did not really love her; that she counted for noth-ing in his life. Yet Sir Hugh had never changed, except that he very seldom made love to her and that she saw less of him than during their engagement. Sir Hugh was still quizzically tender, still all grace, all deference, when he was there. And what wonder that he was little there; he had a wide life; he was a brilliant man; she was a stupid young girl; in looking back, no longer young, no longer stu-pid, Lady Channice thought that she could see it all quite clearly.

She had seemed to him a sweet, good girl, and he cared for her and wanted a wife. He had hoped that by degrees she would grow into a wise and capable woman, fit to help and ornament his life. But she had not been wise or capable. She had been lonely and unhappy, and that wide life of his had wearied and confused her; the silence, the watching attitude of the girl were inadequate to her married state, and yet she had nothing else to meet it with. She had never before felt her youth and inexperience as oppressive, but they oppressed her now. She had nothing to ask of the world and nothing to give to it. What she did ask of life was not given to her, what she had to give was not wanted. She was very unhappy.

Yet people were kind. In especial Lady Elliston was kind, the loveliest, most sheltering, most understanding of all her guests or hostesses. Lady Elliston and her cheerful, jocose husband, were Sir Hugh's nearest friends and they took her in and made much of her. And one day when, in a fit of silly wretchedness, Lady Elliston found her crying, she had put her arms around her and kissed her and begged to know her grief and to comfort it. Even thus taken by surprise, and even to one so kind, Amabel could not tell that grief: deep in her was a reticence, a sense of values austere and immaculate: she could not discuss her husband, even with the kindest of friends. And she had nothing to tell, really, but of herself, her own helplessness and deficiency. Yet, without her telling, for all her wish that no one should guess, Lady Elliston did guess. Her comfort had such wise meaning in it. She was ten years older than Amabel. She knew all about the world; she knew all about girls and their husbands. Amabel was only a girl, and that was the trouble, she seemed to say. When she grew older she would see that it would come right; husbands were always so; the wider life reached by marriage would atone in many ways. And Lady Elliston, all with sweetest discretion, had asked gentle questions. Some of them Amabel had not understood; some she had. She remembered now that her own silence or dull negation might have seemed very rude and ungrateful; yet Lady Elliston had taken no offence. All her memories of Lady Elliston were of this tact and sweetness, this penetrating, tentative tact and sweetness that sought to understand and help and that drew back, unflurried and unprotesting before rebuff, ready to emerge again at any hint of need,—of these, and of her great beauty, the light of her large clear eyes, the whiteness of her throat, the glitter of diamonds about and above: for it was always in her most festal aspect, at night, under chandeliers and in ballrooms, that she best remembered her. Amabel knew, with the deep, instinctive sense of values which was part of her inheritance and hardly, at that time, part of her thought, that her mother would not have liked Lady Elliston, would have thought her worldly; yet, and this showed that Amabel was developing, she had already learned that worldliness was compatible with many things that her mother would have excluded from it; she could see Lady Elliston with her own and with her mother's eyes, and it was puzzling, part of the pain of growth, to feel that her own was already the wider vision.

Soon after that the real story came. The city began to burn and smoke and flames to blind and scorch her.

It was at Lady Elliston's country house that Amabel first met Paul Quentin. He was a daring young novelist who was being made much of during those years; for at that still somewhat guileless time to be daring had been to be original. His books had power and beauty, and he had power and beauty, fierce, dreaming eyes and an intuitive, sudden smile. Under his aspect of careless artist, his head was a little turned by his worldly success, by great country-houses and flattering great ladies; he did not take the world as indifferently as he seemed to. Success edged his self-confidence with a reckless assurance. He was an ardent student of Nietzsche, at a time when that, too, was to be original. Amabel met this young man constantly at the dances and country parties of a season. And, suddenly, the world changed. It was not dawn and it was not daylight; it was a wild and beautiful illumination like torches at night. She knew herself loved and her own being became precious and enchanting to her. The presence of the man who loved her filled her with rapture and fear. Their recognition was swift. He told her things about herself that she had never dreamed of and as he told them she felt them to be true.

To other people Paul Quentin did not speak much of Lady Channice. He early saw that he would need to be discreet. One day at Lady Elliston's her beauty was in question and someone said that she was too pale and too impassive; and at that Quentin, smiling a little fiercely, remarked that she was as pale as a cowslip and as impassive as a young Madonna; the words pictured her; her fresh Spring-like quality, and the peace, as of some noble power not yet roused.

In looking back, it was strange and terrible to Lady Channice to see how little she had really known this man. Their meetings, their talks together, were like the torchlight that flashed and wavered and only fitfully revealed. From the first she had listened, had assented, to everything he said, hanging upon his words and his looks and living afterward in the memory of them. And in memory their significance seemed so to grow that when they next met they found themselves far nearer than the words had left them.

All her young reserves and dignities had been penetrated and dissolved. It was always themselves he talked of, but, from that centre, he waved the torch about a transformed earth and showed her a world of thought and of art that she had never seen before. No murmur of it had reached the deanery; to her husband and the people he lived among it was a mere spectacle; Quentin made that bright, ardent world real to her, and serious. He gave her books to read; he took her to hear music; he showed her the pictures, the statues, the gems and porcelains that she had before accepted as part of the background of life hardly seeing them. From being the background of life they became, in a sense, suddenly its object. But not their object—not his and hers,—though they talked of them, looked, listened and understood. To Quentin and Amabel this beauty was still background, and in the centre, at the core of things, were their two selves and the ecstasy of feeling that exalted and terrified. All else in life became shackles. It was hardly shock, it was more like some immense relief, when, in each other's arms, the words of love, so long implied, were spoken. He said that she must come with him; that she must leave it all and come. She fought against herself and against him in refusing, grasping at pale memories of duty, honour, self-sacrifice; he knew too well the inner treachery that denied her words. But, looking back, trying not to flinch before the scorching memory, she did not know how he had won her. The dreadful jostle of opportune circumstance; her husband's absence, her brother's;—the chance pause in the empty London house between country visits;—Paul Quentin following, finding her there;

the hot, dusty, enervating July day, all seemed to have pushed her to the act of madness and made of it a willess yielding rather than a decision. For she had yielded; she had left her husband's house and gone with him.

They went abroad at once, to France, to the forest of Fontainebleau. How she hated ever after the sound of the lovely syllables, hated the memory of the rocks and woods, the green shadows and the golden lights where she had walked with him and known horror and despair deepening in her heart with every day. She judged herself, not him, in looking back; even then it had been herself she had judged. Though unwilling, she had been as much tempted by herself as by him; he had had to break down barriers, but though they were the barriers of her very soul, her longing heart had pressed, had beaten against them, crying out for deliverance. She did not judge him, but, alone with him in the forest, alone with him in the bland, sunny hotel, alone with him through the long nights when she lay awake and wondered, in a stupor of despair, she saw that he was different. So different; there was the horror. She was the sinner; not he. He belonged to the bright, ardent life, the life without social bond or scruple, the life of sunny, tolerant hotels and pagan forests; but she did not belong to it. The things that had seemed external things, barriers and shackles, were the realest things, were in fact the inner things, were her very self. In yielding to her heart she had destroyed herself, there was no life to be lived henceforth with this man, for there was no self left to live it with. She saw that she had cut herself off from her future as well as from her past. The sacred past judged her and the future was dead. Years of experience concentrated themselves into that lawless week. She saw that laws were not outside things; that they were one's very self at its wisest. She saw that if laws were to be broken it could only be by a self wiser than the self that had made the law. And the self that had fled with Paul Quentin was only a passionate, blinded fragment, a heart without a brain, a fragment judged and rejected by the whole.

To both lovers the week was one of bitter disillusion, though for Quentin no such despair was possible. For him it was an attempt at joy and beauty that had failed. This dulled, drugged looking girl was not the radiant woman he had hoped to find. Vain and sensitive as he was, he felt, almost immediately, that he had lost his charm for her; that she had ceased to love him. That was the ugly, the humiliating side of the truth, the side that so filled Amabel Channice's soul with sickness as she looked back at it. She had ceased to love him, almost at once.

And it was not guilt only, and fear, that had risen between them and separated them; there were other, smaller, subtler reasons, little snakes that hissed in her memory. He was different from her in other ways.

She hardly saw that one of the ways was that of breeding; but she felt that he jarred upon her constantly, in their intimacy, their helpless, dreadful intimacy. In contrast, the thought of her husband had been with her, burningly. She did not say to herself, for she did not know it, her experience of life was too narrow to give her the knowledge,—that her husband was a gentleman and her lover, a man of genius though he were, was not; but she compared them, incessantly, when Quentin's words and actions, his instinctive judgments of men and things, made her shrink and flush. He was so clever, cleverer far than Hugh; but he did not know, as Sir Hugh would have known, what the slight things were that would make her shrink. He took little liberties when he should have been reticent and he was humble when he should have been assured. For he was often humble; he was, oddly, pathetically—and the pity for him added to the sickness—afraid of her and then, because he was afraid, he grew angry with her.

He was clever; but there are some things cleverness cannot reach. What he failed to feel by instinct, he tried to scorn. It was not the patrician scorn, stupid yet not ignoble, for something hardly seen, hardly judged, merely felt as dull and insignificant; it was the corroding plebeian scorn for a suspected superiority.

He quarrelled with her, and she sat silent, knowing that her silence, her passivity, was an affront the more, but helpless, having no word to say. What could she say?—I do love you: I am wretched: utterly wretched and utterly destroyed.—That was all there was to say. So she sat, dully listening, as if drugged. And she only winced when he so far forgot himself as to cry out that it was her silly pride of blood, the aristocratic illusion, that had infected her; she belonged to the caste that could not think and that picked up the artist and thinker to amuse and fill its vacancy. — "We may be lovers, or we may be performing poodles, but we are never equals," he had cried. It was for him Amabel had winced, knowing, without raising her eyes to see it, how his face would burn with humiliation for having so betrayed his consciousness of difference. Nothing that he could say could hurt her for herself.

But there was worse to bear: after the violence of his anger came the violence of his love. She had borne at first, dully, like the slave she felt herself; for she had sold herself to him, given herself over bound hand and foot. But now it became intolerable. She could not protest,—what was there to protest against, or to appeal to?—but she could fly. The thought of flight rose in her after the torpor of despair and, with its sense of wings, it felt almost like a joy. She could fly back, back, to be scourged and purified, and then—oh far away she saw it now—was something beyond despair; life once more; life hidden, crippled, but life. A prayer rose like a sob with the thought.

So one night in London her brother Bertram, coming back late to his rooms, found her sitting there.

Bertram was hard, but not unkind. The sight of her white, fixed face touched him. He did not upbraid her, though for the past week he had rehearsed the bitterest of upbraidings. He even spoke soothingly to her when, speechless, she broke into wild sobs. "There, Amabel, there.—Yes, it's a frightful mess you've made of things.— When I think of mother!—Well, I'll say nothing now. You have come back; that is something. You *have* left him, Amabel?"

She nodded, her face hidden.

"The brute, the scoundrel," said Bertram, at which she moaned a negation.—"You don't still care about him?—Well, I won't question you now.—Perhaps it's not so desperate. Hugh has been very good about it; he's helped me to keep the thing hushed up until we could make sure. I hope we've succeeded; I hope so indeed. Hugh will see you soon, I know; and it can be patched up, no doubt, after a fashion."

But at this Amabel cried:—"I can't.—I can't.—Oh—take me away.—Let me hide until he divorces me. I can't see him."

"Divorces you?" Bertram's voice was sharp. "Have you disgraced publicly—you and us? It's not you I'm thinking of so much as the family name, father and mother. Hugh won't divorce you; he can't; he shan't. After all you're a mere child and he didn't look after you." But this was said rather in threat to Hugh than in leniency to Amabel.

She lay back in the chair, helpless, almost lifeless: let them do with her what they would.

Bertram said that she should spend the night there and that he would see Hugh in the morning. And:—"No; you needn't see him yet, if you feel you can't. It may be arranged without that. Hugh will understand." And this was the first ray of the light that was to grow and grow. Hugh would understand.

She did not see him for two years.

All that had happened after her return to Bertram was a blur now. There were hasty talks, Bertram defining for her her future position, one of dignity it must be—he insisted on that; Hugh perfectly understood her wish for the present, quite fell in with it; but, eventually, she must take her place in her husband's home again. Even Bertram, intent as he was on the family honour, could not force the unwilling wife upon the merely magnanimous husband.

Her husband's magnanimity was the radiance that grew for Amabel during these black days, the days of hasty talks and of her journey down to Charlock House.

She had never seen Charlock House before; Sir Hugh had spoken of the family seat as "a dismal hole," but, on that hot July evening of her arrival, it looked peaceful to her, a dark haven of refuge, like the promise of sleep after nightmare.

Mrs. Bray stood in the door, a grim but not a hostile warder: Amabel felt anyone who was not hostile to be almost kind.

The house had been hastily prepared for her, dining-room and drawing-room and the large bedroom upstairs, having the same outlook over the lawn, the sycamores, the flat meadows. She could see herself standing there now, looking about her at the bedroom where gaiety and gauntness were oddly mingled in the faded carnations and birds of paradise on the chintzes and in the vastness of the four-poster, the towering wardrobes, the capacious, creaking chairs and sofas. Everything was very clean and old; the dressing-table was stiffly skirted in darned muslins and near the pin-cushion stood a small, tight nosegay, Mrs. Bray's cautious welcome to this ambiguous mistress.

"A comfortable old place, isn't it," Bertram had said, looking about, too; "You'll soon get well and strong here, Amabel." This, Amabel knew, was said for the benefit of Mrs. Bray who stood, non-committal and observant just inside the door. She knew, too, that Bertram was depressed by the gauntness and gaiety of the bedroom and even more depressed by the maroon leather furniture and the cases of stuffed birds below, and that he was at once glad to get away from Charlock House and sorry for her that she should have to be left there, alone with Mrs. Bray. But to Amabel it was a dream after a nightmare. A strange, desolate dream, all through those sultry summer days; but a dream shot through with radiance in the thought of the magnanimity that had spared and saved her.

And with the coming of the final horror, came the final revelation of this radiance. She had been at Charlock House for many weeks, and it was mid-Autumn, when that horror came. She knew that she was to have a child and that it could not be her husband's child.

With the knowledge her mind seemed unmoored at last; it wavered and swung in a nightmare blackness deeper than any she had known. In her physical prostration and mental disarray the thought of suicide was with her. How face Bertram now, — Bertram with his tenacious hopes? How face her husband — ever — ever — in the far future? Her disgrace lived and she was to see it. But, in the swinging chaos, it was that thought that kept her from frenzy; the thought that it did live; that its life claimed her; that to it she must atone. She did not love this child that was to come; she dreaded it; yet the dread was sacred, a burden that she must bear for its unhappy sake. What did she not owe to it — unfortunate one — of atonement and devotion?

She gathered all her courage, armed her physical weakness, her wandering mind, to summon Bertram and to tell him.

She told him in the long drawing-room on a sultry September day, leaning her arms on the table by which she sat and covering her face.

Bertram said nothing for a long time. He was still boyish enough to feel any such announcement as embarrassing; and that it should be told him now, in such circumstances, by his sister, by Amabel, was nearly incredible. How associate such savage natural facts, lawless and unappeasable, with that young figure, dressed in its trousseau white muslin and with its crown of innocent gold. It made her suddenly seem older than himself and at once more piteous and more sinister. For a moment, after the sheer stupor, he was horribly angry with her; then came dismay at his own cruelty.

"This does change things, Amabel," he said at last.

"Yes," she answered from behind her hands.

"I don't know how Hugh will take it," said Bertram.

"He must divorce me now," she said. "It can be done very quietly, can't it. And I have money. I can go away, somewhere, out of England—I've thought of America—or New Zealand—some distant country where I shall never be heard of; I can bring up the child there."

Bertram stared at her. She sat at the table, her hands before her face, in the light, girlish dress that hung loosely about her. She was fragile and wasted. Her voice seemed dead. And he wondered at the unhappy creature's courage.

"Divorce!" he then said violently; "No; he can't do that;—and he had forgiven already; I don't know how the law stands; but of course you won't go away. What an idea; you might as well kill yourself outright. It's only—. I don't know how the law stands. I don't know what Hugh will say."

Bertram walked up and down biting his nails. He stopped presently before a window, his back turned to his sister, and, flushing over the words, he said: "You are sure—you are quite sure, Amabel, that it isn't Hugh's child. You are such a girl. You can know nothing.—I mean—it may be a mistake."

"I am quite sure," the unmoved voice answered him. "I do know."

Bertram again stood silent. "Well," he said at last, turning to her though he did not look at her, "all I can do is to see how Hugh takes it. You know, Amabel, that you can count on me. I'll see after you, and after the child. Hugh may, of course, insist on your parting from it; that will probably be the condition he'll make;—naturally. In that case I'll take you abroad soon. It can be got through, I suppose, without anybody knowing; assumed names; some Swiss or Italian village—" Bertram muttered, rather to himself than to her. "Good God, what an odious business!—But, as you say, we have money; that simplifies everything. You mustn't worry about the child. I will see that it is put into safe hands and I'll keep an eye on its future—." He stopped, for his sister's hands had fallen. She was gazing at him, still dully—for it seemed that nothing could strike any excitement from her—but with a curious look, a look that again made him feel as if she were much older than he.

"Never," she said.

"Never what?" Bertram asked. "You mean you won't part from the child?"

"Never; never," she repeated.

"But Amabel," with cold patience he urged; "if Hugh insists.—My poor girl, you have made your bed and you must lie on it. You can't expect your husband to give this child—this illegitimate child—his name. You can't expect him to accept it as his child."

"No; I don't expect it," she said.

"Well, what then? What's your alternative?"

"I must go away with the child."

"I tell you, Amabel, it's impossible," Bertram in his painful anxiety spoke with irritation. "You've got to consider our name—my name, my position, and your husband's. Heaven knows I want to be kind to you—do all I can for you; I've not once reproached you, have I? But you must be reasonable. Some things you must accept as your punishment. Unless Hugh is the most fantastically generous of men you'll have to part from the child."

She sat silent.

"You do consent to that?" Bertram insisted.

She looked before her with that dull, that stupid look. "No," she replied.

Bertram's patience gave way, "You are mad," he said. "Have you no consideration for me—for us? You behave like this—incredibly, in my mother's daughter—never a girl better brought up; you go off with that—that bounder;—you stay with him for a week—good heavens!—there'd have been more dignity if you'd stuck to him;—you chuck him, in one week, and then you come back and expect us to do as you think fit, to let you disappear and everyone know that you've betrayed your husband and had a child by another man. It's mad, I tell you, and it's impossible, and you've got to submit. Do you hear? Will you answer me, I say? Will you promise that if Hugh won't consent to fathering the child—won't consent to giving it his name—won't consent to having it, as his heir, disinherit the lawful children he may have by you—good heavens, I wonder if you realize what you are asking!—will you promise, I say, if he doesn't consent, to part from the child?"

She did look rather mad, her brother thought, and he remembered, with discomfort, that women, at such times, did sometimes lose their reason. Her eyes with their dead gaze nearly frightened him, when, after all his violence, his entreaty, his abuse of her, she only, in an unchanged voice, said "No."

He felt then the uselessness of protestation or threat; she must be treated as if she were mad; humored, cajoled. He was silent for a little while, walking up and down. "Well, I'll say no more, then. Forgive me for my harshness," he said. "You give me a great deal to bear, Amabel; but I'll say nothing now. I have your word, at all events," he looked sharply at her as the sudden suspicion crossed him, "I have your word that you'll stay quietly here—until you hear from me what Hugh says? You promise me that?"

"Yes," his sister answered. He gave a sigh for the sorry relief.

That night Amabel's mind wandered wildly. She heard herself, in the lonely room where she lay, calling out meaningless things. She tried to control the horror of fear that rose in her and peopled the room with phantoms; but the fear ran curdling in her veins and flowed about her, shaping itself in forms of misery and disaster. "No—no—poor child.—Oh—don't—don't.—I will come to you. I am your mother.—They can't take you from me."—this was the most frequent cry.

The poor child hovered, wailing, delivered over to vague, unseen sorrow, and, though a tiny infant, it seemed to be Paul Quentin, too, in some dreadful plight, appealing to her in the name of their dead love to save him. She did not love him; she did not love the child; but her heart seemed broken with impotent pity.

In the intervals of nightmare she could look, furtively, fixedly, about the room. The moon was bright outside, and through the curtains a pallid light showed the menacing forms of the two great wardrobes. The four posts of her bed seemed like the pillars of some vast, alien temple, and the canopy, far above her, floated like a threatening cloud. Opposite her bed, above the chimney-piece, was a deeply glimmering mirror: if she were to raise herself she would see her own white reflection, rising, ghastly.—She hid her face on her pillows and sank again into the abyss.

Next morning she could not get up. Her pulses were beating at fever speed; but, with the daylight, her mind was clearer. She could summon her quiet look when Mrs. Bray came in to ask her mournfully how she was. And a little later a telegram came, from Bertram.

Her trembling hands could hardly open it. She read the words. "All is well." Mrs. Bray stood beside her bed. She meant to keep that quiet look for Mrs. Bray; but she fainted. Mrs. Bray, while she lay tumbled among the pillows, and before lifting her, read the message hastily.

From the night of torment and the shock of joy, Amabel brought an extreme susceptibility to emotion that showed itself through all her life in a trembling of her hands and frame when any stress of feeling was laid upon her.

After that torment and that shock she saw Bertram once, and only once, again;—ah, strange and sad in her memory that final meeting of their lives, though this miraculous news was the theme of it. She was still in bed when he came, the bed she did not leave for months, and, though so weak and dizzy, she understood all that he told her, knew the one supreme fact of her husband's goodness. He sent her word that she was to be troubled about nothing; she was to take everything easily and naturally. She should always have her child with her and it should bear his name. He would see after it like a father; it should never know that he was not its father. And, as soon as she would let him, he would come and see her—and it. Amabel, lying on her pillows, gazed and gazed: her eyes, in their shadowy hollows, were two dark wells of sacred wonder. Even Bertram felt something of the wonder of them. In his new gladness and relief, he was very kind to her. He came and kissed her. She seemed, once more, a person whom one could kiss. "Poor dear," he said, "you have had a lot to bear. You do look dreadfully ill. You must get well and strong, now, Amabel, and not worry any more, about anything. Everything is all right. We will call the child Augustine, if it's a boy, after mother's father you know, and Katherine, if it's a girl, after her mother: I feel, don't you, that we have no right to use their own names. But the further away ones seem right, now. Hugh is a trump, isn't he? And, I'm sure of it, Amabel, when time has passed a little, and you feel you can, he'll have you back; I do really believe it may be managed. This can all be explained. I'm saying that you are ill, a nervous breakdown, and are having a complete rest."

She heard him dimly, feeling these words irrelevant. She knew that Hugh must never have her back; that she could never go back to Hugh; that her life henceforth was dedicated. And yet Bertram was kind, she felt that, though dimly feeling, too, that her old image of him had grown tarnished. But her mind was far from Bertram and the mitigations he offered. She was fixed on that radiant figure, her husband, her knight, who had stooped to her in her abasement, her agony, and had lifted her from dust and darkness to the air where she could breathe,—and bless him.

"Tell him—I bless him,"—she said to Bertram. She could say nothing more. There were other memories of that day, too, but even more dim, more irrelevant. Bertram had brought papers for her to sign, saying: "I know you'll want to be very generous with Hugh now," and she had raised herself on her elbow to trace with the fingers that trembled the words he dictated to her.

There was sorrow, indeed, to look back on after that. Poor Bertram died only a month later, struck down by an infectious illness. He was not to see or supervise the rebuilding of his sister's shattered life, and the anguish in her sorrow was the thought of all the pain that she had brought to his last months of life: but this sorrow, after the phantoms, the nightmares, was like the weeping of tears after a dreadful weeping of blood. Her tears fell as she lay there, propped on her pillows—for she was very ill—and looking out over the Autumn fields; she wept for poor Bertram and all the pain; life was sad. But life was good and beautiful. After the flames, the suffocation, it had brought her here, and it showed her that radiant figure, that goodness and beauty embodied in human form. And she had more to help her, for he wrote to her, a few delicately chosen words, hardly touching on their own case, his and hers, but about her brother's death and of how he felt for her in her bereavement, and of what a friend dear Bertram had been to himself. "Some day, dear Amabel, you must let me come and see you" it ended; and "Your affectionate husband."

It was almost too wonderful to be borne. She had to close her eyes in thinking of it and to lie very still, holding the blessed letter in her hand and smiling faintly while she drew long soft breaths. He was always in her thoughts, her husband; more, far more, than her coming child. It was her husband who had made that coming a thing possible to look forward to with resignation; it was no longer the nightmare of desolate flights and hidings.

And even after the child was born, after she had seen its strange little face, even then, though it was all her life, all her future, it held the second place in her heart. It was her life, but it was from her husband that the gift of life had come to her.

She was a gentle, a solicitous, a devoted mother. She never looked at her baby without a sense of tears. Unfortunate one, was her thought, and the pulse of her life was the yearning to atone.

She must be strong and wise for her child and out of her knowledge of sin and weakness in herself must guide and guard it.

But in her yearning, in her brooding thought, was none of the mother's rapturous folly and gladness. She never kissed her baby. Some dark association made the thought of kisses an unholy thing and when, forgetting, she leaned to it sometimes, thoughtless, and delighting in littleness and sweetness, the dark memory of guilt would rise between its lips and hers, so that she would grow pale and draw back.

When first she saw her husband, Augustine was over a year old. Sir Hugh had written and asked if he might not come down one day and spend an hour with her. "And let all the old fogies see that we are friends," he said, in his remembered playful vein.

It was in the long dark drawing-room that she had seen him for the first time since her flight into the wilderness.

He had come in, grave, yet with something blithe and unperturbed in his bearing that, as she stood waiting for what he might say to her, seemed the very nimbus of chivalry. He was splendid to look at, too, tall and strong with clear kind eyes and clear kind smile.

She could not speak, not even when he came and took her hand, and said: "Well Amabel." And then, seeing how white she was and how she trembled, he had bent his head and kissed her hand. And at that she had broken into tears; but they were tears of joy.

He stood beside her while she wept, her hands before her face, just touching her shoulder with a paternal hand, and she heard him saying: "Poor little Amabel: poor little girl."

She took her chair beside the table and for a long time she kept her face hidden: "Thank you; thank you;" was all that she could say.

"My dear, what for?—There, don't cry.—You have stopped crying? There, poor child. I've been awfully sorry for you."

He would not let her try to say how good he was, and this was a relief, for she knew that she could not put it into words and that, without words, he understood. He even laughed a little, with a graceful embarrassment, at her speechless gratitude. And presently, when they talked, she could put down her hand, could look round at him, while she answered that, yes, she was very comfortable at

Charlock House; yes, no place could suit her more perfectly; yes, Mrs. Bray was very kind.

And he talked a little about business with her, explaining that Bertram's death had left him with a great deal of management on his hands; he must have her signature to papers, and all this was done with the easiest tact so that naturalness and simplicity should grow between them; so that, in finding pen and papers in her desk, in asking where she was to sign, in obeying the pointing of his finger here and there, she should recover something of her quiet, and be able to smile, even, a little answering smile, when he said that he should make a business woman of her. And—"Rather a shame that I should take your money like this, Amabel, but, with all Bertram's money, you are quite a bloated capitalist. I'm rather hard up, and you don't grudge it, I know."

She flushed all over at the idea, even said in jest:—"All that I have is yours."

"Ah, well, not all," said Sir Hugh. "You must remember—other claims." And he, too, flushed a little now in saying, gently, tentatively;—"May I see the little boy?"

"I will bring him," said Amabel.

How she remembered, all her life long, that meeting of her husband and her son. It was the late afternoon of a bright June day and the warm smell of flowers floated in at the open windows of the drawing-room. She did not let the nurse bring Augustine, she carried him down herself. He was a large, robust baby with thick, corn-coloured hair and a solemn, beautiful little face. Amabel came in with him and stood before her husband holding him and looking down. Confusion was in her mind, a mingling of pride and shame.

Sir Hugh and the baby eyed each other, with some intentness. And, as the silence grew a little long, Sir Hugh touched the child's cheek with his finger and said: "Nice little fellow: splendid little fellow. How old is he, Amabel? Isn't he very big?"

"A year and two months. Yes, he is very big."

"He looks like you, doesn't he?"

"Does he?" she said faintly.

"Just your colour," Sir Hugh assured her. "As grave as a little king, isn't he. How firmly he looks at me."

"He is grave, but he never cries; he is very cheerful, too, and well and strong."

"He looks it. He does you credit. Well, my little man, shall we be friends?" Sir Hugh held out his hand. Augustine continued to gaze at him, unmoving. "He won't shake hands," said Sir Hugh.

Amabel took the child's hand and placed it in her husband's; her own fingers shook. But Augustine drew back sharply, doubling his arm against his breast, though not wavering in his gaze at the stranger.

Sir Hugh laughed at the decisive rejection. "Friendship's on one side, till later," he said.

When her husband had gone Amabel went out into the sycamore wood. It was a pale, cool evening. The sun had set and the sky beyond the sycamores was golden. Above, in a sky of liquid green, the evening star shone softly.

A joy, sweet, cold, pure, like the evening, was in her heart. She stopped in the midst of the little wood among the trees, and stood still, closing her eyes.

Something old was coming back to her; something new was being given. The memory of her mother's eyes was in it, of the simple prayers taught her by her mother in childhood, and the few words, rare and simple, of the presence of God in the soul. But her girlish prayer, her girlish thought of God, had been like a thread-like, singing brook. What came to her now grew from the brook-like running of trust and innocence to a widening river, to a sea that filled her, over-flowed her, encompassed her, in whose power she was weak, through whose power her weakness was uplifted and made strong.

It was as if a dark curtain of fear and pain lifted from her soul, showing vastness, and deep upon deep of stars. Yet, though this that came to her was so vast, it made itself small and tender, too, like the flowers glimmering about her feet, the breeze fanning her hair and garments, the birds asleep in the branches above her. She held out her hands, for it seemed to fall like dew, and she smiled, her face uplifted.

She did not often see her husband in the quiet years that followed. She did not feel that she needed to see him. It was enough to know that he was there, good and beautiful.

She knew that she idealised him, that in ordinary aspects he was a happy, easy man-of-the-world; but that was not the essential; the essential in him was the pity, the tenderness, the comprehension that had responded to her great need. He was very unconscious of aims or ideals; but when the time for greatness came he showed it as naturally and simply as a flower expands to light. The thought of him henceforth was bound up with the thought of her religion; nothing of rapture or ecstasy was in it; it was quiet and grave, a revelation of holiness.

It was as if she had been kneeling to pray, alone, in a dark, devastated church, trembling, and fearing the darkness, not daring to approach the unseen altar; and that then her husband's hand had lighted all the high tapers one by one, so that the church was filled with radiance and the divine made manifest to her again.

Light and quietness were to go with her, but they were not to banish fear. They could only help her to live with fear and to find life beautiful in spite of it.

For if her husband stood for the joy of life, her child stood for its sorrow. He was the dark past and the unknown future. What she should find in him was unrevealed; and though she steadied her soul to the acceptance of whatever the future might bring of pain for her, the sense of trembling was with her always in the thought of what it might bring of pain for Augustine.

IV

L ady Channice woke on the morning after her long retrospect bringing from her dreams a heavy heart.

She lay for some moments after the maid had drawn her curtains, looking out at the fields as she had so often looked, and wondering why her heart was heavy. Throb by throb, like a leaden shuttle, it seemed to weave together the old and new memories, so that she saw the pattern of yesterday and of today, Lady Elliston's coming, the pain that Augustine had given her in his strange questionings, the meeting of her husband and her son. And the ominous rhythm of the shuttle was like the footfall of the past creeping upon her.

It was more difficult than it had been for years, this morning, to quiet the throb, to stay her thoughts on strength. She could not pray, for her thoughts, like her heart, were leaden; the whispered words carried no message as they left her lips; she could not lift her thought to follow them. It was upon a lesser, a merely human strength, that she found herself dwelling. She was too weak, too troubled, to find the swiftness of soul that could soar with its appeal, the stillness of soul where the divine response could enter; and weakness turned to human help. The thought of her husband's coming was like a glow of firelight seen at evening on a misty moor. She could hasten towards it, quelling fear. There she would be safe. By his mere presence he would help and sustain her. He would be kind and tactful with Augustine, as he had always been; he would make a shield between her and Lady Elliston. She could see no sky above, and the misty moor loomed with uncertain shapes; but she could look before her and feel that she went towards security and brightness.

Augustine and his mother both studied during the day, the same studies, for Lady Channice, to a great extent, shared her son's scholarly pursuits. From his boyhood—a studious, grave, yet violent little boy he had been, his fits of passionate outbreak quelled, as he grew older, by the mere example of her imperturbability beside him—she had thus shared everything. She had made herself his tutor as well as his guardian angel. She was more tutor, more guardian angel, than mother.

Their mental comradeship was full of mutual respect. And though Augustine was not of the religious temperament, though his mother's instinct told her that in her lighted church he would be a respectful looker-on rather than a fellow-worshipper, though they never spoke of religion, just as they seldom kissed, Augustine's growing absorption in metaphysics tinged their friendship with a religious gravity and comprehension.

On three mornings in the week Lady Channice had a class for the older village girls; she sewed, read and talked with them, and was fond of them all. These girls, their placing in life, their marriages and babies, were her most real interest in the outer world. During the rest of the day she gardened, and read whatever books Augustine might be reading. It was the mother and son's habit thus to work apart and to discuss work in the evenings.

Today, when her girls were gone, she found herself very lonely. Augustine was out riding and in her room she tried to occupy herself, fearing her own thoughts. It was past twelve when she heard the sound of his horse's hoofs on the gravel before the door and, throwing a scarf over her hair, she ran down to meet him.

The hall door at Charlock House, under a heavy portico, looked out upon a circular gravel drive bordered by shrubberies and enclosed by high walls; beyond the walls and gates was the high-road. An interval of sunlight had broken into the chill Autumn day: Augustine had ridden bareheaded and his gold hair shone as the sun fell upon it. He looked, in his stately grace, like an equestrian youth on a Greek frieze. And, as was usual with his mother, her appreciation of Augustine's nobility and fineness passed at once into a pang: so beautiful; so noble; and so shadowed. She stood, her black scarf about her face and shoulders, and smiled at him while he threw the reins to the old groom and dismounted.

"Nice to find you waiting for me," he said. "I'm late this morning. Too late for any work before lunch. Don't you want a little walk? You look pale."

"I should like it very much. I may miss my afternoon walk—your father may have business to talk over."

They went through the broad stone hall-way that traversed the house and stepped out on the gravel walk at the back. This path, running below the drawing-room and dining-room windows, led down on one side to the woods, on the other to Lady Channice's garden, and was a favourite place of theirs for quiet saunterings. Today the sunlight fell mildly on it. A rift of pale blue showed in the still grey sky.

"I met Marjory," said Augustine, "and we had a gallop over Pangley Common. She rides well, that child. We jumped the hedge and ditch at the foot of the common, you know — the high hedge — for practice. She goes over like a bird."

Amabel's mind was dwelling on the thought of shadowed brightness and Marjory, fresh, young, deeply rooted in respectability, seemed suddenly more significant than she had ever been before. In no way Augustine's equal, of course, except in that impersonal, yet so important matter of roots; Amabel had known a little irritation over Mrs. Grey's open manoeuvreings; but on this morning of rudderless tossing, Marjory appeared in a new aspect. How sound; how safe. It was of Augustine's insecurity rather than of Augustine himself that she was thinking as she said: "She is such a nice girl."

"Yes, she is," said Augustine.

"What did you talk about?"

"Oh, the things we saw; birds and trees and clouds. — I pour information upon her."

"She likes that, one can see it."

"Yes, she is so nice and guileless that she doesn't resent my pedantry. I love giving information, you know," Augustine smiled. He looked about him as he spoke, at birds and trees and clouds, happy, humorous, clasping his riding crop behind his back so that his mother heard it make a pleasant little click against his gaiter as he walked.

"It's delightful for both of you, such a comradeship."

"Yes; a comradeship after a fashion; Marjory is just like a nice little boy."

"Ah, well, she is growing up; she is seventeen, you know. She is more than a little boy."

"Not much; she never will be much more."

"She will make a very nice woman."

Augustine continued to smile, partly at the thought of Marjory, and partly at another thought. "You mustn't make plans, for me and Marjory, like Mrs. Grey," he said presently. "It's mothers like Mrs.

Grey who spoil comradeships. You know, I'll never marry Marjory. She is a nice little boy, and we are friends; but she doesn't interest me."

"She may grow more interesting: she is so young. I don't make plans, dear,—yet I think that it might be a happy thing for you."

"She'll never interest me," said Augustine.

"Must you have a very interesting wife?"

"Of course I must:—she must be as interesting as you are!" he turned his head to smile at her.

"You are not exacting, dear!"

"Yes, I am, though. She must be as interesting as you—and as good; else why should I leave you and go and live with someone else.—Though for that matter, I shouldn't leave you. You'd have to live with us, you know, if I ever married."

"Ah, my dear boy," Lady Channice murmured. She managed a smile presently and added: "You might fall in love with someone not so interesting. You can't be sure of your feelings and your mind going together."

"My feelings will have to submit themselves to my mind. I don't know about 'falling'; I rather dislike the expression: one might 'fall' in love with lots of people one would never dream of marrying. It would have to be real love. I'd have to love a woman very deeply before I wanted her to share my life, to be a part of me; to be the mother of my children." He spoke with his cheerful gravity.

"You have an old head on very young shoulders, Augustine."

"I really believe I have!" he accepted her somewhat sadly humorous statement; "and that's why I don't believe I'll ever make a mistake. I'd rather never marry than make a mistake. I know I sound priggish; but I've thought a good deal about it: I've had to." He paused for a moment, and then, in the tone of quiet, unconfused confidence that always filled her with a sense of mingled pride and humility, he added:—"I have strong passions, and I've already seen what happens to people who allow feeling to govern them."

Amabel was suddenly afraid. "I know that you would always be—good Augustine; I can trust you for that." She spoke faintly.

They had now walked down to the little garden with its box borders and were wandering vaguely among the late roses. She paused to look at the roses, stooping to breathe in the fragrance of a tall white cluster: it was an instinctive impulse of hiding: she hoped in another moment to find an escape in some casual gardening remark. But Augustine, unsuspecting, was interested in their theme.

"Good? I don't know," he said. "I don't think it's goodness, exactly. It's that I so loathe the other thing, so loathe the animal I know in myself, so loathe the idea of life at the mercy of emotion."

She had to leave the roses and walk on again beside him, steeling herself to bear whatever might be coming. And, feeling that unconscious accusation loomed, she tried, as unconsciously, to mollify and evade it.

"It isn't always the animal, exactly, is it?—or emotion only? It is romance and blind love for a person that leads people astray."

"Isn't that the animal?" Augustine inquired. "I don't think the animal base, you know, or shameful, if he is properly harnessed and kept in his place. It's only when I see him dominating that I hate and fear him so. And," he went on after a little pause of reflection, "I especially hate him in that form;—romance and blind love: because what is that, really, but the animal at its craftiest and most dangerous? what is romance—I mean romance of the kind that jeopardizes 'goodness'—what is it but the most subtle self-deception? You don't love the person in the true sense of love; you don't want their good; you don't want to see them put in the right relation to their life as a whole:—what you want is sensation through them; what you want is yourself in them, and their absorption in you. I don't think that wicked, you know—I'm not a monk or even a puritan—if it's the mere result of the right sort of love, a happy glamour that accompanies, the right sort; it's in its place, then, and can endanger nothing. But people are so extraordinarily blind about love; they don't seem able to distinguish between the real and the false. People usually, though they don't know it, mean only desire when they talk of love."

There was another pause in which she wondered that he did not hear the heavy throbbing of her heart. But now there was no retreat; she must go on; she must understand her son. "Desire must enter in," she said.

"In its place, yes; it's all a question of that;" Augustine replied, smiling a little at her, aware of the dogmatic flavour of his own utterances, the humorous aspect of their announcement, to her, by him;—"You love a woman enough and respect her enough to wish her to be the mother of your children—assuming, of course, that you consider yourself worthy to carry on the race; and to think of a woman in such a way is to feel a rightful emotion and a rightful desire; anything else makes emotion the end instead of the result and is corrupting, I'm sure of it."

"You have thought it all out, haven't you"; Lady Channice steadied her voice to say. There was panic rising in her, and a strange anger made part of it.

"I've had to, as I said," he replied. "I'm anything but self-controlled by nature; already," and Augustine looked calmly at his mother, "I'd have let myself go and been very dissolute unless I'd had this ideal of my own honour to help me. I'm of anything but a saintly disposition."

"My dear Augustine!" His mother had coloured faintly. Absurd as it was, when the reality of her own life was there mocking her, the bald words were strange to her.

"Do I shock you?" he asked. "You know I always feel that you *are* a saint, who can hear and understand everything."

She blushed deeply, painfully, now. "No, you don't shock me;—I am only a little startled."

"To hear that I'm sensual? The whole human race is far too sensual in my opinion. They think a great deal too much about their sexual appetites;—only they don't think about them in those terms unfortunately; they think about them veiled and wreathed; that's why we are sunk in such a bog of sentimentality and sin."

Lady Channice was silent for a long time. They had left the garden, and walked along the little path near the sunken wall at the foot of the lawn, and, skirting the wood of sycamores, had come back to the broad gravel terrace. A turmoil was in her mind; a longing to know and see; a terror of what he would show her.

"Do you call it sin, that blinded love? Do you think that the famous lovers of romance were sinners?" she asked at last; "Tristan and Iseult? — Abélard and Héloise? — Paolo and Francesca?"

"Of course they were sinners," said Augustine cheerfully. "What did they want? — a present joy: purely and simply that: they sacrificed everything to it — their own and other people's futures: what's that but sin? There is so much mawkish rubbish talked and written about such persons. They were pathetic, of course, most sinners are; that particular sin, of course, may be so associated and bound up with beautiful things; — fidelity, and real love may make such a part of it, that people get confused about it."

"Fidelity and real love?" Lady Channice repeated: "you think that they atone — if they make part of an illicit passion?"

"I don't think that they atone; but they may redeem it, mayn't they? Why do you ask me?" Augustine smiled; — "You know far more about these things than I do."

She could not look at him. His words in their beautiful unconsciousness appalled her. Yet she had to go on, to profit by her own trance-like strength. She was walking on the verge of a precipice but she knew that with steady footsteps she could go towards her appointed place. She must see just where Augustine put her, just how he judged her.

"You seem to know more than I do, Augustine," she said: "I've not thought it out as you have. And it seems to me that any great emotion is more of an end in itself than you would grant. But if the illicit passion thinks itself real and thinks itself enduring, and proves neither, what of it then? What do you think of lovers to whom that happens? It so often happens, you know."

Augustine had his cheerful answer ready. "Then they are stupid as well as sinful. Of course it is sinful to be stupid. We've learned that from Plato and Hegel, haven't we?"

The parlour-maid came out to announce lunch. Lady Channice was spared an answer. She went to her room feeling shattered, as if great stones had been hurled upon her.

Yes, she thought, gazing at herself in the mirror, while she untied her scarf and smoothed her hair, yes, she had never yet, with all her agonies of penitence, seen so clearly what she had been: a sinner: a stupid sinner. Augustine's rigorous young theories might set too inhuman an ideal, but that aspect of them stood out clear: he had put, in bald, ugly words, what, in essence, her love for Paul Quentin had been: he had stripped all the veils and wreaths away. It had been self; self, blind in desire, cruel when blindness left it: there had been no real love and no fidelity to redeem the baseness. A stupid sinner; that, her son had told her, was what she had been. The horror of it smote back upon her from her widened, mirrored eyes, and she sat for a moment thinking that she must faint.

Then she remembered that Augustine was waiting for her downstairs and that in little more than an hour her husband would be with her. And suddenly the agony lightened. A giddiness of relief came over her. He was kind: he did not judge her: he knew all, yet he respected her. Augustine was like the bleak, stony moor; she must shut her eyes and stumble on towards the firelight. And as she thought of that nearing brightness, of her husband's eyes, that never judged, never grew hard or fierce or remote from human tolerance, a strange repulsion from her son rose in her. Cold, fierce, righteous boy; cold, heartless theories that one throb of human emotion would rightly shatter;—the thought was almost like an echo of Paul Quentin speaking in her heart to comfort her. She sprang up: that was indeed the last turn of horror. If she was not to faint she must not think. Action alone could dispel the whirling mist where she did not know herself.

She went down to the dining-room. Augustine stood looking out of the window. "Do come and see this delightful swallow," he said: "he's skimming over and over the lawn."

She felt that she could not look at the swallow. She could only walk to her chair and sink down on it. Augustine repelled her with his cheerfulness, his trivial satisfactions. How could he not know that she was in torment and that he had plunged her there. This involuntary injustice to him was, she saw again, veritably crazed.

She poured herself out water and said in a voice that surprised herself:—"Very delightful, I am sure; but come and have your lunch. I am hungry."

"And how pale you are," said Augustine, going to his place. "We stayed out too long. You got chilled." He looked at her with the solicitude that was like a brother's—or a doctor's. That jarred upon her racked nerves, too.

"Yes; I am cold," she said.

She took food upon her plate and pretended to eat. Augustine, she guessed, must already feel the change in her. He must see that she only pretended. But he said nothing more. His tact was a further turn to the knot of her sudden misery.

Augustine was with her in the drawing-room when she heard the wheels of the station-fly grinding on the gravel drive; they sounded very faintly in the drawing-room, but, from years of listening, her hearing had grown very acute.

She could never meet her husband without an emotion that betrayed itself in pallor and trembling and today the emotion was so marked that Augustine's presence was at once a safeguard and an anxiety; before Augustine she could be sure of not breaking down, not bursting into tears of mingled gladness and wretchedness, but though he would keep her from betraying too much to Sir Hugh, would she not betray too much to him? He was reading a review and laid it down as the door opened: she could only hope that he noticed nothing.

Sir Hugh came in quickly. At fifty-four he was still a very handsome man of a chivalrous and soldierly bearing. He had long limbs, broad shoulders and a not yet expanded waist. His nose and chin were clearly and strongly cut, his eyes brightly blue; his moustache ran to decisive little points twisted up from the lip and was as decorative as an epaulette upon a martial shoulder. Pleasantness radiated from him, and though, with years, this pleasantness was significant rather of his general attitude than of his individual interest, though his movements had become a little indolent and his features a little heavy, these changes, to affectionate eyes, were merely towards a more pronounced geniality and contentedness.

Today, however, geniality and contentment were less apparent. He looked slightly nipped and hardened, and, seeming pleased to find a fire, he stood before it, after he had shaken hands with his wife and with Augustine, and said that it had been awfully cold in the train.

"We will have tea at half past four instead of five today, then," said Amabel.

But no, he replied, he couldn't stop for tea: he must catch the four-four back to town: he had a dinner and should only just make it.

His eye wandered a little vaguely about the room, but he brought it back to Amabel to say with a smile that the fire made up for the loss of tea. There was then a little silence during which it might have been inferred that Sir Hugh expected Augustine to leave the room. Amabel, too, expected it; but Augustine had taken up his review and was reading again. She felt her fear of him, her anger against him, grow.

Very pleasantly, Sir Hugh at last suggested that he had a little business to talk over. "I think I'll ask Augustine to let us have a half hour's talk."

"Oh, I'll not interfere with business," said Augustine, not lifting his eyes.

The silence, now, was more than uncomfortable; to Amabel it was suffocating. She could guess too well that some latent enmity was expressed in Augustine's assumed unconsciousness. That Sir Hugh was surprised, displeased, was evident; but, when he spoke again, after a little pause, it was still pleasantly:—"Not with business, but with talk you will interfere. I'm afraid I must ask you.—I don't often have a chance to talk with your mother.—I'll see you later, eh?"

Augustine made no reply. He rose and walked out of the room.

Sir Hugh still stood before the fire, lifting first the sole of one boot and then the other to the blaze. "Hasn't always quite nice manners, has he, the boy"; he observed. "I didn't want to have to send him out, you know."

"He didn't realize that you wanted to talk to me alone." Amabel felt herself offering the excuse from a heart turned to stone.

"Didn't he, do you think? Perhaps not. We always do talk alone, you know. He's just a trifle tactless, shows a bit of temper sometimes. I've noticed it. I hope he doesn't bother you with it."

"No. I never saw him like that, before," said Amabel, looking down as she sat in her chair.

"Well, that's all that matters," said Sir Hugh, as if satisfied.

His boots were quite hot now and he went to the writing-desk drawing a case of papers from his breast-pocket.

"Here are some of your securities, Amabel," he said: "I want a few more signatures. Things haven't been going very well with me lately. I'd be awfully obliged if you'd help me out."

"Oh—gladly—" she murmured. She rose and came to the desk. She hardly saw the papers through a blur of miserable tears while she wrote her name here and there. She was shut out in the mist and dark; he wasn't thinking of her at all; he was chill, preoccupied; something was displeasing him; decisively, almost sharply, he told her where to write. "You mustn't be worried, you know," he observed as he pointed out the last place; "I'm arranging here, you see, to pass Charlock House over to you for good. That is a little return for all you've done. It's not a valueless property. And then Bertram tied up a good sum for the child, you know."

His speaking of "the child," made her heart stop beating, it brought the past so near.—And was Charlock House to be her very own? "Oh," she murmured, "that is too good of you.—You mustn't do that.—Apart from Augustine's share, all that I have is yours; I want no return."

"Ah, but I want you to have it"; said Sir Hugh; "it will ease my conscience a little. And you really do care for the grim old place, don't you."

"I love it."

"Well, sign here, and here, and it's yours. There. Now you are mistress in your own home. You don't know how good you've been to me, Amabel."

The voice was the old, kind voice, touched even, it seemed, with an unwonted feeling, and, suddenly, the tears ran down her cheeks as, looking at the papers that gave her her home, she said, faltering:—"You are not displeased with me?—Nothing is the matter?"

He looked at her, startled, a little confused. "Why my dear girl,—displeased with you?—How could I be?—No. It's only these confounded affairs of mine that are in a bit of a mess just now."

"And can't I be of even more help—without any returns? I can be so economical for myself, here. I need almost nothing in my quiet life."

Sir Hugh flushed. "Oh, you've not much more to give, my dear. I've taken you at your word."

"Take me completely at my word. Take everything."

"You dear little saint," he said. He patted her shoulder. The door was wide; the fire shone upon her. She felt herself falling on her knees before it, with happy tears. He, who knew all, could say that to her, with sincerity. The day of lowering fear and bewilderment opened to sudden joy. His hand was on her shoulder; she lifted it and kissed it.

"Oh! Don't!"—said Sir Hugh. He drew his hand sharply away. There was confusion, irritation, in his little laugh.

Amabel's tears stood on scarlet cheeks. Did he not understand?—Did he think?—And was he right in thinking?—Shame flooded her. What girlish impulse had mingled incredibly with her gratitude, her devotion?

Sir Hugh had turned away, and as she sat there, amazed with her sudden suspicion, the door opened and Augustine came in saying:—"Here is Lady Elliston, Mother."

V

L ady Elliston helped her. How that, too, brought back the past to Amabel as she rose and moved forward, before her husband and her son, to greet the friend of twenty years ago.

Lady Elliston, at difficult moments, had always helped her, and this was one of the most difficult that she had ever known. Amabel forgot her tears, forgot her shame, in her intense desire that Augustine should guess nothing.

"My very dear Amabel," said Lady Elliston. She swept forward and took both Lady Channice's hands, holding them firmly, looking at her intently, intently smiling, as if, with her own mastery of the situation, to give her old friend strength. "My dear, dear Amabel," she repeated: "How good it is to see you again.—And how lovely you are."

She was silken, she was scarfed, she was soft and steady; as in the past, sweetness and strength breathed from her. She was competent to deal with most calamitous situations and to make them bearable, to make them even graceful. She could do what she would with situations: Amabel felt that of her now as she had felt it years ago.

Her eyes continued to gaze for a long moment into Amabel's eyes before, as softly and as steadily, they passed to Sir Hugh who was again standing before the fire behind his wife. "How do you do," she then said with a little nod.

"How d'ye do," Sir Hugh replied. His voice was neither soft nor steady; the sharpness, the irritation was in it. "I didn't know you were down here," he said.

Over Amabel's shoulder, while she still held Amabel's hands, Lady Elliston looked at him, all sweetness. "Yes: I arrived this morning. I am staying with the Greys."

"The Greys? How in the dickens did you run across them?" Sir Hugh asked with a slight laugh.

"I met them at Jack's cousin's—the nice old bishop, you know. They are tiresome people; but kind. And there is a Grey *fils*—the oldest—whom Peggy took rather a fancy to last winter,—they were hunting together in Yorkshire;—and I wanted to look at him—and at the place!—"—Lady Elliston's smile was all candour. "They are very solid; it's not a bad place. If the young people are really serious Jack and I might consider it; with three girls still to marry, one must be very wise and reasonable. But, of course, I came really to see you, Amabel."

She had released Amabel's hands at last with a final soft pressure, and, as Amabel took her accustomed chair near the table, she sat down near her and loosened her cloak and unwound her scarf, and threw back her laces.

"And I've been making friends with your boy," she went on, looking up at Augustine: — "he's been walking me about the garden, saying that you mustn't be disturbed. Why haven't I been able to make friends before? Why hasn't he been to see me in London?"

"I'll bring him someday," said Sir Hugh. "He is only just grown up, you see."

"I see: do bring him soon. He is charming," said Lady Elliston, smiling at Augustine.

Amabel remembered her pretty, assured manner of saying any pleasantness — or unpleasantness for that matter — that she chose to say; but it struck her, from this remark, that the gift had grown a little mechanical. Augustine received it without embarrassment. Augustine already seemed to know that this smiling guest was in the habit of saying that young men were charming before their faces when she wanted to be pleasant to them. Amabel seemed to see her son from across the wide chasm that had opened between them; but, looking at his figure, suddenly grown strange, she felt that Augustine's manners were 'nice.' The fact of their niceness, of his competence — really it matched Lady Elliston's — made him the more mature; and this moment of motherly appreciation led her back to the stony wilderness where her son judged her, with a man's, not a boy's judgment. There was no uncertainty in Augustine; his theories might be young; his character was formed; his judgments would not change. She forced herself not to think; but to look and listen.

Lady Elliston continued to talk: indeed it was she and Augustine who did most of the talking. Sir Hugh only interjected a remark now and then from his place before the fire. Amabel was able to feel a further change in him; he was displeased today, and displeased in particular, now, with Lady Elliston. She thought that she could understand the vexation for him of this irruption of his real life into the sad little corner of kindness and duty that Charlock House and its occupants must represent to him. He had seldom spoken to her about Lady Elliston; he had seldom spoken to her about any of the life that she had abandoned in abandoning him: but she knew that Lord and Lady Elliston were near friends still, and with this knowledge she could imagine how on edge her husband must be when to the near friend of the real life he could allow an even sharper note to alter all his voice. Amabel heard it sadly, with a sense of confused values: nothing today was as she had expected it to be: and if she heard she was sure that Lady Elliston must hear it too, and perhaps the symptom of Lady Elliston's displeasure was that she talked rather pointedly to Augustine and talked hardly at all to Sir Hugh: her eyes, in speaking, passed sometimes over his figure, rested sometimes, with a bland courtesy, on his face when he spoke; but Augustine was their object: on him they dwelt and smiled.

The years had wrought few changes in Lady Elliston. Silken, soft, smiling, these were, still, as in the past, the words that described her. She had triumphantly kept her lovely figure: the bright brown hair, too, had been kept, but at some little sacrifice of sincerity: Lady Elliston must be nearly fifty and her shining locks showed no sign of fading. Perhaps, in the perfection of her appearance and manner, there was a hint of some sacrifice everywhere. How much she has kept, was the first thought; but the second came:—How much she has given up. Yes; there was the only real change: Amabel, gazing at her, somewhat as a nun gazes from behind convent gratings at some bright denizen of the outer world, felt it more and more. She was sweet, but was she not too skilful? She was strong, but was not her strength unscrupulous? As she listened to her, Amabel remembered old wonders, old glimpses of motives that stole forth reconnoitring and then retreated at the hint of rebuff, graceful and unconfused.

There were motives now, behind that smile, that softness; motives behind the flattery of Augustine, the blandness towards Sir Hugh, the visit to herself. Some of the motives were, perhaps, all kindness: Lady Elliston had always been kind; she had always been a binder of wounds, a dispenser of punctual sunlight, she was one of the world's powerfully benignant great ladies; committees clustered round her; her words of assured wisdom sustained and guided ecclesiastical and political organisations; one must be benignant, in an altruistic modern world, if one wanted to rule. It was not a cynical nun who gazed; Lady Elliston was kind and Lady Elliston loved power; simply, without a sense of blame, Amabel drew her conclusions.

There were now lapses in Lady Elliston's fluency. Her eyes rested contemplatively on Amabel; it was evident that she wanted to see Amabel alone. This motive was so natural a one that, although Sir Hugh seemed determined, at the risk of losing his train, to stay till the last minute, he, too, felt, at last, its pressure.

His wife saw him go with a sense of closing mists. Augustine, now more considerate, followed him. She was left facing her guest.

Only Lady Elliston could have kept the moment from being openly painful and even Lady Elliston could not pretend to find it an easy one; but she did not err on the side of too much tact. It was so sweetly, so gravely that her eyes rested for a long moment of silence on her old friend, so quietly that they turned away from her rising flush, that Amabel felt old gratitudes mingling with old distrusts.

"What a sad room this is," said Lady Elliston, looking about it. "Is it just as you found it, Amabel?"

"Yes, almost. I have taken away some things."

"I wish you would take them all away and put in new ones. It might be made into a very nice room; the panelling is good. What it needs is Jacobean furniture, fine old hangings, and some bits of glass and porcelain here and there."

"I suppose so." Amabel's eyes followed Lady Elliston's. "I never thought of changing anything."

Lady Elliston's eyes turned on hers again. "No: I suppose not," she said.

She seemed to find further meanings in the speech and took it up again with: "I suppose not. It's strange that we should never have met in all these years, isn't it."

"Is it strange?"

"I've often felt it so: if you haven't, that is just part of your acceptance. You have accepted everything. It has often made me indignant to think of it."

Amabel sat in her high-backed chair near the table. Her hands were tightly clasped together in her lap and her face, with the light from the windows falling upon it, was very pale. But she knew that she was calm; that she could meet Lady Elliston's kindness with an answering kindness; that she was ready, even, to hear Lady Elliston's questions. This, however, was not a question, and she hesitated for a moment before saying: "I don't understand you."

"How well I remember that voice," Lady Elliston smiled a little sadly: "It's the girl's voice of twenty years ago—holding me away. Can't we be frank together, now, Amabel, when we are both middle-aged women?—at least I am middle-aged.—How it has kept you young, this strange life you've led."

"But, really, I do not understand," Amabel murmured, confused; "I didn't understand you then, sometimes."

"Then I may be frank?"

"Yes; be frank, of course."

"It is only that indignation that I want to express," said Lady Elliston, tentative no longer and firmly advancing. "Why are you here, in this dismal room, this dismal house? Why have you let yourself be cloistered like this? Why haven't you come out and claimed things?"

Amabel's grey eyes, even in their serenity always a little wild, widened with astonishment. "Claimed?" she repeated. "What do you mean? What could I have claimed? I have been given everything."

"My dear Amabel, you speak as if you had deserved this imprisonment."

There was another and a longer silence in which Amabel seemed slowly to find meanings incredible to her before. And her reception of them was expressed in the changed, the hardened voice with which she said: "You know everything. I've always been sure you knew. How can you say such things to me?"

"Do not be angry with me, dear Amabel. I do not mean to offend."

"You spoke as though you were sorry for me, as though I had been injured.—It touches him."

"But," Lady Elliston had flushed very slightly, "it does touch him. I blame Hugh for this. He ought not to have allowed it. He ought not to have accepted such misplaced penitence. You were a mere child, and Hugh neglected you shamefully."

"I was not a mere child," said Amabel. "I was a sinful woman."

Lady Elliston sat still, as if arrested and spell-bound by the unexpected words. She seemed to find no answer. And as the silence grew long, Amabel went on, slowly, with difficulty, yet determinedly opposing and exposing the folly of the implied accusation. "You don't seem to remember the facts. I betrayed my husband. He might have cast me off. He might have disgraced me and my child. And he lifted me up; he sheltered me; he gave his name to the child. He has given me everything I have. You see—you must not speak of him like that to me."

Lady Elliston had gathered herself together though still, it was evident, bewildered. "I don't mean to blame Hugh so much. It was your fault, too, I suppose. You asked for the cloister, I know."

"No; I didn't ask for it. I asked to be allowed to go away and hide myself. The cloister, too, was a gift,—like my name, my undishonoured child."

"Dear, dear Amabel," said Lady Elliston, gazing at her, "how beautiful of you to be able to feel like that."

"It isn't I who am beautiful"; Amabel's lips trembled a little now and her eyes filled suddenly with tears. Tears and trembling seemed to bring hardness rather than softening to her face; they were like a chill breeze, like an icy veil, and the face, with its sorrow, was like a winter's landscape.

"He is so beautiful that he would never let anyone know or understand what I owe him: he would never know it himself: there is something simple and innocent about such men: they do beautiful things unconsciously. You know him well: you are far nearer him than I am: but you can't know what the beauty is, for you have never been helpless and disgraced and desperate nor needed anyone to lift you up. No one can know as I do the angel in my husband."

Lady Elliston sat silent. She received Amabel's statements steadily yet with a little wincing, as though they had been bullets whistling past her head; they would not pierce, if one did not move; yet an involuntary compression of the lips and flutter of the eyelids revealed a rather rigid self-mastery. Only after the silence had grown long did she slightly stir, move her hand, turn her head with a deep, careful breath, and then say, almost timidly; "Then, he has lifted you up, Amabel?—You are happy, really happy, in your strange life?"

Amabel looked down. The force of her vindicating ardour had passed from her. With the question the hunted, haunted present flooded in. Happy? Yesterday she might have answered "yes," so far away had the past seemed, so forgotten the fear in which she had learned to breathe. Today the past was with her and the fear pressed heavily upon her heart. She answered in a sombre voice: "With my past what woman could be happy. It blights everything."

"Oh—but Amabel—" Lady Elliston breathed forth. She leaned forward, then moved back, withdrawing the hand impulsively put out.—"Why?—Why?—" she gently urged. "It is all over: all passed: all forgotten. Don't—ah don't let it blight anything."

"Oh no," said Amabel, shaking her head. "It isn't over; it isn't forgotten; it never will be. Hugh cannot forget—though he has forgiven. And someday, I feel it, Augustine will know. Then I shall drink the cup of shame to the last drop."

"Oh!—" said Lady Elliston, as if with impatience. She checked herself. "What can I say?—if you will think of yourself in this preposterous way.—As for Augustine, he does not know and how should he ever know? How could he, when no one in the world knows but you and I and Hugh."

She paused at that, looking at Amabel's downcast face. "You notice what I say, Amabel?"

"Yes; that isn't it. He will guess."

"You are morbid, my poor child.—But do you notice nothing when I say that only we three know?"

Amabel looked up. Lady Elliston met her eyes. "I came today to tell you, Amabel. I felt sure you did not know. There is no reason at all, now, why you should dread coming out into the world—with Augustine. You need fear no meetings. You did not know that he was dead."

"He?"

"Yes. He. Paul Quentin."

Amabel, gazing at her, said nothing.

"He died in Italy, last week. He was married, you know, quite happily; an ordinary sort of person; she had money; he rather let his work go. But they were happy; a large family; a villa on a hill somewhere; pictures, bric-à-brac and bohemian intellectualism. You knew of his marriage?"

"Yes; I knew."

The tears had risen to Lady Elliston's eyes before that stricken, ashen face; she looked away, murmuring: "I wanted to tell you, when we were alone. It might have come as such an ugly shock, if you were unprepared. But, now, there is no danger anymore. And you will come out, Amabel?"

"No;—never.—It was never that."

"But what was it then?"

Amabel had risen and was looking around her blindly.

"It was.—I have no place but here.—Forgive me—I must go. I can't talk any more."

"Yes; go; do go and lie down." Lady Elliston, rising too, put an arm around her shoulders and took her hand. "I'll come again and see you. I am going up to town for a night or so on Tuesday, but I bring Peggy down here for the next week-end. I'll see you then.— Ah, here is Augustine, and tea. He will give me my tea and you must sleep off your headache. Your poor mother has a very bad headache, Augustine. I have tried her. Goodbye, dear, go and rest."

VI

A n hour ago Augustine had found his mother in tears; now he found her beyond them. He gave her his arm, and, outside in the hall, prepared to mount the stairs with her; but, shaking her head, trying, with miserable unsuccess, to smile, she pointed him back to the drawing-room and to his duties of host.

"Ah, she is very tired. She does not look well," said Lady Elliston. "I am glad to see that you take good care of her."

"She is usually very well," said Augustine, standing over the tea-tray that had been put on the table between him and Lady Elliston. "Let's see: what do you have? Sugar? milk?"

"No sugar; milk, please. It's such a great pleasure to me to meet your mother again."

Augustine made no reply to this, handing her her cup and the plate of bread and butter.

"She was one of the loveliest girls I have ever seen," Lady Elliston went on, helping herself. "She looked like a Madonna—and a cowslip.—And she looks like that more than ever." She had paused for a moment as an uncomfortable recollection came to her. It was Paul Quentin who had said that: at her house.

"Yes," Augustine assented, pleased, "she does look like a cowslip; she is so pale and golden and tranquil. It's funny you should say so," he went on, "for I've often thought it; but with me it's an association of ideas, too. Those meadows over there, beyond our lawn, are full of cowslips in Spring and ever since I can remember we have picked them there together."

"How sweet"; Lady Elliston was still a little confused, by her blunder, and by his words. "What a happy life you and your mother must have had, cloistered here. I've been telling your mother that it's like a cloister. I've been scolding her a little for shutting herself up in it. And now that I have this chance of talking to you I do very much want to say that I hope you will bring her out a little more."

"Bring her out? Where?" Augustine inquired.

"Into the world—the world she is so fitted to adorn. It's ridiculous this—this fad of hers," said Lady Elliston.

"Is it a fad?" Augustine asked, but with at once a lightness and distance of manner.

"Of course. And it is bad for anyone to be immured."

"I don't think it has been bad for her. Perhaps this is more the world than you think."

"I only mean bad in the sense of sad."

"Isn't the world sad?"

"What a strange young man you are. Do you really mean to say that you like to see your mother—your beautiful, lovely mother—imprisoned in this gloomy place and meeting nobody from one year's end to the other?"

"I have said nothing at all about my likes," said Augustine, smiling.

Lady Elliston gazed at him. He startled her almost as much as his mother had done. What a strange young man, indeed; what strange echoes of his father and mother in him. But she had to grope for the resemblances to Paul Quentin; they were there; she felt them; but they were difficult to see; while it was easy to see the resemblances to Amabel. His father was like a force, a fierceness in him, controlled and guided by an influence that was his mother. And where had he found, at nineteen, that assurance, an assurance without his father's vanity or his mother's selflessness? Paul Quentin had been assured because he was so absolutely sure of his own value; Amabel was assured because, in her own eyes, she was valueless; this young man seemed to be without self-reference or self-effacement; but he was quite self-assured. Had he some mental talisman by which he accurately gauged all values, his own included? He seemed at once so oddly above yet of the world. She pulled herself together to remember that he was, only, nineteen, and that she had had motives in coming, and that if these motives had been good they were now better.

"You have said nothing; but I am going to ask you to say something"; she smiled back at him. "I am going to ask you to say that you will take me on trust. I am your friend and your mother's friend."

"Since when, my mother's?" Augustine asked. His amiability of aspect remained constant.

"Since twenty years."

"Twenty years in which you have not seen your friend."

"I know that that looks strange. But when one shuts oneself away into a cloister one shuts out friends."

"Does one?"

"You won't trust me?"

"I don't know anything about you, except that you have made my mother ill and that you want something of me."

"My dear young man I, at all events, know one thing about you very clearly, and that is that I trust you."

"I want nothing of you," said Augustine, but he still smiled, so that his words did not seem discourteous.

"Nothing? Really nothing? I am your mother's friend, and you want nothing of me? I have sought her out; I came today to see and understand; I have not made her ill; she was nearly crying when we came into the room, you and I, a little while ago. What I see and understand makes me sad and angry. And I believe that you, too, see and understand; I believe that you, too, are sad and angry. And I want to help you. I want you, when you come into the world, as you must, to bring your mother. I'll be waiting there for you both. I am a sort of fairy-godmother. I want to see justice done."

"I suppose you mean that you are angry with my father and want to see justice done on him," said Augustine after a pause.

Again Lady Elliston sat suddenly still, as if another, an unexpected bullet, had whizzed past her. "What makes you say that?" she asked after a moment.

"What you have said and what you have seen. He had been making her cry," said Augustine. He was still calm, but now, under the calm, she heard, like the thunder of the sea in caverns deep beneath a placid headland, the muffled sound of a hidden, a dark indignation.

"Yes," she said, looking into his eyes; "that made me angry; and that he should take all her money from her, as I am sure he does, and leave her to live like this."

Augustine's colour rose. He turned away his eyes and seemed to ponder.

"I do want something of you, after all; the answer to one question," he said at last. "Is it because of him that she is cloistered here?"

In a flash Lady Elliston had risen to her emergency, her opportunity. She was grave, she was ready, and she was very careful.

"It was her own choice," she said.

Augustine pondered again. He, too, was grave and careful She saw how, making use of her proffered help, he yet held her at a distance. "That does not answer my question," he said. "I will put it in another way. Is it because of some evil in his life that she is cloistered?"

Lady Elliston sat before him in one of the high-backed chairs; the light was behind her: the delicate oval of her face maintained its steady attitude: in the twilit room Augustine could see her eyes fixed very strangely upon him. She, too, was perhaps pondering. When at last she spoke, she rose in speaking, as if her answer must put an end to their encounter, as if he must feel, as well as she, that after her answer there could be no further question.

"Not altogether, for that," she said; "but, yes, in part it is because of what you would call an evil in his life that she is cloistered."

Augustine walked with her to the door and down the stone passage outside, where a strip of faded carpet hardly kept one's feet from the cold. He was nearer to her in this curious moment of their parting than he had been at all. He liked Lady Elliston in her last response; it was not the wish to see justice wreaked that had made it; it was mere truth.

When they had reached the hall door, he opened it for her and in the fading light he saw that she was very pale. The Grey's dog-cart was going slowly round and round the gravel drive. Lady Elliston did not look at him. She stood waiting for the groom to see her.

"What you asked me was asked in confidence," she said; "and what I have told you is told in confidence."

"It wasn't new to me; I had guessed it," said Augustine. "But your confirmation of what I guessed is in confidence."

"I have been your father's life-long friend," said Lady Elliston; "He is not an evil man."

"I understand. I don't misjudge him."

"I don't want to see justice done on him," said Lady Elliston. The groom had seen her and the dog-cart, with a brisk rattle of wheels, drew up to the door. "It isn't a question of that; I only want to see justice done *for* her."

All through she had been steady; now she was sweet again. "I want to free her. I want you to free her. And — whenever you do — I shall be waiting to give her to the world again."

They looked at each other now and Augustine could answer, with another smile; "You are the world, I suppose."

"Yes; I am the world," she accepted. "The actual fairy-godmother, with a magic wand that can turn pumpkins into coaches and put Cinderellas into their proper places."

Augustine had handed her up to her seat beside the groom. He tucked her rug about her. If he had laid aside anything to meet her on her own ground, he, too, had regained it now.

"But does the world always know what *is* the proper place?" was his final remark as she drove off.

She did not know that she could have found an answer to it.

VII

A mabel was sitting beside her window when her son came in and the face she turned on him was white and rigid.

"My dear mother," said Augustine, coming up to her, "how pale you are."

She had been sitting there for all that time, tearless, in a stupor of misery. Yes, she answered him, she was very tired.

Augustine stood over her looking out of the window. "A little walk wouldn't do you good?" he asked.

No, she answered, her head ached too badly.

She could find nothing to say to him: the truth that lay so icily upon her heart was all that she could have said: "I am your guilty mother. I robbed you of your father. And your father is dead, unmourned, unloved, almost forgotten by me." For that was the poison in her misery, to know that for Paul Quentin she felt almost nothing. To hear that he had died was to hear that a ghost had died.

What would Augustine say to her if the truth were spoken? It was now a looming horror between them. It shut her from him and it shut him away.

"Oh, do come out," said Augustine after a moment: "the evening's so fine: it will do you good; and there's still a bit of sunset to be seen."

She shook her head, looking away from him.

"Is it really so bad as that?"

"Yes; very bad."

"Can't I do anything? Get you anything?"

"No, thank you."

"I'm so sorry," said Augustine, and, suddenly, but gravely, deliberately, he stooped and kissed her.

"Oh—don't!—don't!" she gasped. She thrust him away, turning her face against the chair. "Don't: you must leave me.—I am so unhappy."

The words sprang forth: she could not repress them, nor the gush of miserable tears.

If Augustine was horrified he was silent. He stood leaning over her for a moment and then went out of the room.

She lay fallen in her chair, weeping convulsively. The past was with her; it had seized her and, in her panic-stricken words, it had thrust her child away. What would happen now? What would Augustine say? What would he ask? If he said nothing and asked nothing, what would he think?

She tried to gather her thoughts together, to pray for light and guidance; but, like a mob of blind men locked out from sanctuary, the poor, wild thoughts only fled about outside the church and fumbled at the church door. Her very soul seemed shut against her.

She roused herself at last, mechanically telling herself that she must go through with it; she must dress and go down to dinner and she must find something to say to Augustine, something that would make what had happened to them less sinister and inexplicable.

—Unless—it seemed like a mad cry raised by one of the blind men in the dark,—unless she told him all, confessed all; her guilt, her shame, the truths of her blighted life. She shuddered; she cowered as the cry came to her, covering her ears and shutting it out. It was mad, mad. She had not strength for such a task, and if that were weakness—oh, with a long breath she drew in the mitigation—if it were weakness, would it not be a cruel, a heartless strength that could blight her child's life too, in the name of truth. She must not listen to the cry. Yet strangely it had echoed in her, almost as if from within, not from without, the dark, deserted church; almost as if her soul, shut in there in the darkness, were crying out to her. She turned her mind from the sick fancy.

Augustine met her at dinner. He was pale but he seemed composed. They spoke little. He said, in answer to her questioning, that he had quite liked Lady Elliston; yes, they had had a nice talk; she seemed very friendly; he should go and see her when he next went up to London.

Amabel felt the crispness in his voice but, centered as she was in her own self-mastery, she could not guess at the degree of his.

After dinner they went into the drawing-room, where the old, ugly lamp added its light to the candles on the mantel-piece.

Augustine took his book and sat down at one side of the table. Amabel sat at the other. She, too, took a book and tried to read; a little time passed and then she found that her hands were trembling so much that she could not. She slid the book softly back upon the table, reaching out for her work-bag. She hoped Augustine had not seen, but, glancing up at him, she saw his eyes upon her.

Augustine's eyes looked strange tonight. The dark rims around the iris seemed to have expanded. Suddenly she felt horribly afraid of him.

They gazed at each other, and she forced herself to a trembling, meaningless smile. And when she smiled at him he sprang up and came to her. He leaned over her, and she shrank back into her chair, shutting her eyes.

"You must tell me the truth," said Augustine. "I can't bear this. *He* has made you unhappy. — *He* comes between us."

She lay back in the darkness, hearing the incredible words.

"He? — What do you mean?"

"He is a bad man. And he makes you miserable. And you love him."

She heard the nightmare: she could not look at it.

"My husband bad? He is good, more good than you can guess. What do you mean by speaking so?"

With closed eyes, shutting him out, she spoke, anger and terror in her voice.

Augustine lifted himself and stood with his hands clenched looking at her.

"You say that because you love him. You love him more than anything or anyone in the world."

"I do. I love him more than anyone or anything in the world. How have you dared — in silence — in secret — to nourish these thoughts against the man who has given you all you have."

"He hasn't given me all I have. You are everything in my life and he is nothing. He is selfish. He is sensual. He is stupid. He doesn't know what beauty or goodness is. I hate him," said Augustine.

Her eyes at last opened on him. She grasped her chair and raised herself. Whose hands were these, desecrating her holy of holies. Her son's? Was it her son who spoke these words? An enemy stood before her.

"Then you do not love me. If you hate him you do not love me," — her anger had blotted out her fear, but she could find no other than these childish words and the tears ran down her face.

"And if you love him you cannot love me," Augustine answered. His self-mastery was gone. It was a fierce, wild anger that stared back at her. His young face was convulsed and livid.

"It is you who are bad to have such false, base thoughts!" his mother cried, and her eyes in their indignation, their horror, struck at him, accused him, thrust him forth. "You are cruel—and hard—and self-righteous.—You do not love me.—There is no tenderness in your heart!"—

Augustine burst into tears. "There is no room in your heart for me!—" he gasped. He turned from her and rushed out of the room.

A long time passed before she leaned forward in the chair where she had sat rigidly, rested her elbows on her knees, buried her face in her hands.

Her heart ached and her mind was empty: that was all she knew. It had been too much. This torpor of sudden weakness was merciful. Now she would go to bed and sleep.

It took her a long time to go upstairs; her head whirled, and if she had not clung to the baluster she would have fallen.

In the passage above she paused outside Augustine's door and listened. She heard him move inside, walking to his window, to lean out into the night, probably, as was his wont. That was well. He, too, would sleep presently.

In her room she said to her maid that she did not need her. It took her but a few minutes tonight to prepare for bed. She could not even braid her uncoiled hair. She tossed it, all loosened, above her head as she fell upon the pillow.

She heard, for a little while, the dull thumping of her heart. Her breath was warm in a mesh of hair beneath her cheek; she was too sleepy to put it away. She was wakened next morning by the maid. Her curtains were drawn and a dull light from a rain-blotted world was in the room.

The maid brought a note to her bedside. From Mr. Augustine, she said.

Amabel raised herself to hold the sheet to the light and read:—

"Dear mother," it said. "I think that I shall go and stay with Wallace for a week or so. I shall see you before I go up to Oxford. Try to forgive me for my violence last night. I am sorry to have added to your unhappiness. Your affectionate son—Augustine."

Her mind was still empty. "Has Mr. Augustine gone?" she asked the maid.

"Yes, ma'am; he left quite early, to catch the eight-forty train."

"Ah, yes," said Amabel. She sank back on her pillow. "I will have my breakfast in bed. Tea, please, only, and toast."—Then, the long habit of self-discipline asserting itself, the necessity for keeping strength, if it were only to be spent in suffering:—"No, coffee, and an egg, too."

She found, indeed, that she was very hungry; she had eaten nothing yesterday. After her bath and the brushing and braiding of her hair, it was pleasant to lie propped high on her pillows and to drink her hot coffee. The morning papers, too, were nice to look at, folded on her tray. She did not wish to read them; but they spoke of a firmly established order, sustaining her life and assuring her of ample pillows to lie on and hot coffee to drink, assuring her that bodily comforts were pleasant whatever else was painful. It was a childish, a still stupefied mood, she knew, but it supported her; an oasis of the familiar, the safe, in the midst of whirling, engulfing storms.

It supported her through the hours when she lay, with closed eyes, listening to the pour and drip of the rain, when, finally deciding to get up, she rose and dressed very carefully, taking all her time.

Below, in the drawing-room, when she entered, it was very dark. The fire was unlit, the bowls of roses were faded; and sudden, childish tears filled her eyes at the desolateness. On such a day as this Augustine would have seen that the fire was burning, awaiting her. She found matches and lighted it herself and the reluctantly creeping brightness made the day feel the drearier; it took a long time even to warm her foot as she stood before it, leaning her arm on the mantel-piece.

It was Saturday; she should not see her girls today; there was relief in that, for she did not think that she could have found anything to say to them this morning.

Looking at the roses again, she felt vexed with the maid for having left them there in their melancholy. She rang and spoke to her almost sharply telling her to take them away, and when she had gone felt the tears rise with surprise and compunction for the sharpness.

There would be no fresh flowers in the room today, it was raining too hard. If Augustine had been here he would have gone out and found her some wet branches of beech or sycamore to put in the vases: he knew how she disliked a flowerless, leafless room, a dislike he shared.

How the rain beat down. She stood looking out of the window at the sodden earth, the blotted shapes of the trees. Beyond the nearest meadows it was like a grey sheet drawn down, confusing earth and sky and shutting vision into an islet.

She hoped that Augustine had taken his mackintosh. He was very forgetful about such things. She went out to look into the bleak, stone hall hung with old hunting prints that were dimmed and spotted with age and damp. Yes, it was gone from its place, and his ulster, too. It had been a considered, not a hasty departure. A tweed cloak that he often wore on their walks hung there still and, vaguely, as though she sought something, she turned it, looked at it, put her hands into the worn, capacious pockets. All were empty except one where she found some withered gorse flowers. Augustine was fond of stripping off the golden blossoms as they passed a bush, of putting his nose into the handful of fragrance, and then holding it out for her to smell it, too:—"Is it apricots, or is it peaches?" she could hear him say.

She went back into the drawing-room holding the withered flowers. Their fragrance was all gone, but she did not like to burn them. She held them and bent her face to them as she stood again looking out. He would by now have reached his destination. Wallace was an Eton friend, a nice boy, who had sometimes stayed at Charlock House. He and Augustine were perhaps already arguing about Nietzsche.

Strange that her numbed thoughts should creep along this path of custom, of maternal associations and solicitudes, forgetful of fear and sorrow. The recognition came with a sinking pang. Reluctantly, unwillingly, her mind was forced back to contemplate the catastrophe that had befallen her. He was her judge, her enemy: yet, on this dismal day, how she missed him. She leaned her head against the window-frame and the tears fell and fell.

If he were there, could she not go to him and take his hand and say that, whatever the deep wounds they had dealt each other, they needed each other too much to be apart. Could she not ask him to take her back, to forgive her, to love her? Ah—there full memory rushed in. Her heart seemed to pant and gasp in the sudden coil. Take him back? When it was her steady fear as well as her sudden anger that had banished him, he thought he loved her, but that was because he did not know and it was the anger rather than the love of Augustine's last words that came to her. He loved her because he believed her good, and that imaginary goodness cast a shadow on her husband. To believe her good Augustine had been forced to believe evil of the man she loved and to whom they both owed everything.

He had said that he was shut out from her heart, and it was true, and her heart broke in seeing it. But it was by more than the sacred love for her husband that her child was shut out. Her past, her guilt, was with her and stood as a barrier between them. She was separated from him for ever. And, looking round the room, suddenly terrified, it seemed to her that Augustine was dead and that she was utterly alone.

VIII

S he did not write to Augustine for some days. There seemed nothing that she could say. To say that she forgave him might seem to put aside too easily the deep wrong he had done her and her husband; to say that she longed to see him and that, in spite of all, her heart was his, seemed to make deeper the chasm of falseness between them.

The rain fell during all these days. Sometimes a pale evening sunset would light the western horizon under lifted clouds and she could walk out and up and down the paths, among her sodden rose-trees, or down into the wet, dark woods. Sometimes at night she saw a melancholy star shining here and there in the vaporous sky. But in the morning the grey sheet dropped once more between her and the outer world, and the sound of the steady drip and beat was like an outer echo to her inner wretchedness.

It was on the fourth day that wretchedness turned to bitter restlessness, and that to a sudden resolve. Not to write, not even to say she forgave, might make him think that her heart was still hardened against him. Her fear had blunted her imagination. Clearly now she saw, and with an anguish in the vision, that Augustine must be suffering too. Clearly she heard the love in his parting words. And she longed so to see, to hear that love again, that the longing, as if with sudden impatience of the hampering sense of sin, rushed into words that might bring him.

She wrote: — "My dear Augustine. I miss you very much. Isn't this dismal weather. I am feeling better. I need not tell you that I do forgive you for the mistake that hurts us both." Then she paused, for her heart cried out "Oh — come back soon"; but she did not dare yield to that cry. She hardly knew that, with uncertain fingers, she only repeated again: — "I miss you very much. Your affectionate mother."

This was on the fourth day.

On the afternoon of the fifth she stood, as she so often stood, looking out at the drawing-room window. She was looking and listening, detached from what she saw, yet absorbed, too, for, as with her son, this watchfulness of natural things was habitual to her.

It was still raining, but more fitfully: a wind had risen and against a scudding sky the sycamores tossed their foliage, dark or pale by turns as the wind passed over them. A broad pool of water, dappling incessantly with raindrops, had formed along the farther edge of the walk where it slanted to the lawn: it was this pool that Amabel was watching and the bobbin-like dance of drops that looked like little glass thimbles. The old leaden pipes, curiously moulded, that ran down the house beside the windows, splashed and gurgled loudly. The noise of the rushing, falling water shut out other sounds. Gazing at the dancing thimbles she was unaware that someone had entered the room behind her.

Suddenly two hands were laid upon her shoulders.

The shock, going through her, was like a violent electric discharge. She tingled from head to foot, and almost with terror. "Augustine!" she gasped. But the shock was to change, yet grow, as if some alien force had penetrated her and were disintegrating every atom of her blood.

"No, not Augustine," said her husband's voice: "But you can be glad to see me, can't you, Amabel?"

He had taken off his hands now and she could turn to him, could see his bright, smiling face looking at her, could feel him as something wonderful and radiant filling the dismal day, filling her dismal heart, with its presence. But the shock still so trembled in her that she did not move from her place or speak, leaning back upon the window as she looked at him,—for he was very near,—and putting her hands upon the window-sill on either side. "You didn't expect to see me, did you," Sir Hugh said.

She shook her head. Never, never, in all these years, had he come again, so soon. Months, always, sometimes years, had elapsed between his visits.

"The last time didn't count, did it," he went on, in speech vague and desultory yet, at the same time, intent and bright in look. "I was so bothered; I behaved like a selfish brute; I'm sure you felt it. And you were so particularly kind and good—and dear to me, Amabel."

She felt herself flushing. He stood so near that she could not move forward and he must read the face, amazed, perplexed, incredulous of its joy, yet all lighted from his presence, that she kept fixed on him. For ah, what joy to see him, to feel that here, here alone of all the world, was she safe, consoled, known yet cared for. He who understood all as no one else in the world understood, could stand and smile at her like that.

"You look thin, and pale, and tired," were his next words. "What have you been doing to yourself? Isn't Augustine here? You're not alone?"

"Yes; I am alone. Augustine is staying with the Wallace boy."

With the mention of Augustine the dark memory came, but it was now of something dangerous and hostile shut away, yes, safely shut away, by this encompassing brightness, this sweetness of intent solicitude. She no longer yearned to see Augustine.

Sir Hugh looked at her for some moments, when, she said that she was alone, without speaking. "That is nice for me," he then said. "But how miserable,—for you,—it must have been. What a shame that you should have been left alone in this dull place,—and this wretched weather, too!—Did you ever see such weather." He looked past her at the rain.

"It has been wretched," said Amabel; but she spoke, as she felt, in the past: nothing seemed wretched now.

"And you were staring out so hard, that you never heard me," He came beside her now, as if to look out, too, and, making room for him, she also turned and they looked out at the rain together.

"A filthy day," said Sir Hugh, "I can't bear to think that this is what you have been doing, all alone."

"I don't mind it, I have the girls, on three mornings, you know."

"You mean that you don't mind it because you are so used to it?"

She had regained some of her composure:—for one thing he was beside her, no longer blocking her way back into the room. "I like solitude, you know," she was able to smile.

"Really like it?"

"Sometimes."

"Better than the company of some people, you mean?"

"Yes."

"But not better than mine," he smiled back. "Come, do encourage me, and say that you are glad to see me."

In her joy the bewilderment was growing, but she said that, of course, she was glad to see him.

"I've been so bored, so badgered," said Sir Hugh, stretching himself a little as though to throw off the incubus of tiresome memories;

"and this morning when I left a dull country house, I said to myself: Why not go down and see Amabel?—I don't believe she will mind.—I believe that, perhaps, she'll be pleased.—I know that I want to go very much.—So here I am:—very glad to be here—with dear Amabel."

She looked out, silent, blissful, and perplexed.

He was not hard; he was not irritated; all trace of vexed preoccupation was gone; but he was not the Sir Hugh that she had seen for all these twenty years. He was new, and yet he reminded her of something, and the memory moved towards her through a thick mist of years, moved like a light through mist. Far, sweet, early things came to her as its heralds; the sound of brooks running; the primrose woods where she had wandered as a girl; the singing of prophetic birds in Spring. The past had never come so near as now when Sir Hugh—yes, there it was, the fair, far light—was making her remember their long past courtship. And a shudder of sweetness went through her as she remembered, of sweetness yet of unutterable sadness, as though something beautiful and dead had been shown to her. She seemed to lean, trembling, to kiss the lips of a beautiful dead face, before drawing over it the shroud that must cover it for ever.

Sir Hugh was silent also. Her silence, perhaps, made him conscious of memories. Presently, looking behind them, he said:—"I'm keeping you standing. Shall we go to the fire?"

She followed him, bending a little to the fire, her arm on the mantel-shelf, a hand held out to the blaze. Sir Hugh stood on the other side. She was not thinking of herself, hardly of him. Suddenly he took the dreaming hand, stooped to it, and kissed it. He had released it before she had time to know her own astonishment.

"You did kiss mine, you know," he smiled, leaning his arm, too, on the mantel-shelf and looking at her with gaily supplicating eyes. "Don't be angry."

The shroud had dropped: the past was gone: she was once more in the present of oppressive, of painful joy.

She would have liked to move away and take her chair at some distance; but that would have looked like flight; foolish indeed. She summoned her common-sense, her maturity, her sorrow, to smile back, to say in a voice she strove to make merely light: "Unusual circumstances excused me."

"Unusual circumstances?"

"You had been very kind. I was very grateful."

Sir Hugh for a moment was silent, looking at her with his intent, interrogatory gaze. "You are always kind to me," he then said. "I am always grateful. So may I always kiss your hand?"

Her eyes fell before his. "If you wish to," she answered gravely.

"You frighten me a little, do you know," said Sir Hugh. "Please don't frighten me. — Are you really angry? — *I* don't frighten you?"

"You bewilder me a little," Amabel murmured. She looked into the fire, near tears, indeed, in her bewilderment; and Sir Hugh looked at her, looked hard and carefully, at her noble figure, her white hands, the gold and white of her leaning head. He looked, as if measuring the degree of his own good fortune.

"You are so lovely," he then said quietly.

She blushed like a girl.

"You are the most beautiful woman I know," said Sir Hugh. "There is no one like you," He put his hand out to hers, and, helplessly, she yielded it. "Amabel, do you know, I have fallen in love with you."

She stood looking at him, stupefied; her eyes ecstatic and appalled.

"Do I displease you?" asked Sir Hugh.

She did not answer.

"Do I please you?" Still she gazed at him, speechless.

"Do you care at all for me?" he asked, and, though grave, he smiled a little at her in asking the question. How could he not know that, for years, she had cared for him more than for anything, anyone?

And when he asked her this last question, the oppression was too great. She drew her hand from his, and laid her arms upon the mantel-shelf and hid her face upon them. It was a helpless confession. It was a helpless appeal.

But the appeal was not understood, or was disregarded. In a moment her husband's arms were about her.

This was new. This was not like their courtship.—Yet, it reminded her,—of what did it remind her as he murmured words of victory, clasped her and kissed her? It reminded her of Paul Quentin. In the midst of the amazing joy she knew that the horror was as great.

"Ah don't!—how can you!—how can you!" she said.

She drew away from him but he would not let her go.

"How can I? How can I do anything else?" he laughed, in easy yet excited triumph. "You do love me—you darling nun!"

She had freed her hands and covered her face: "I beg of you," she prayed.

The agony of her sincerity was too apparent. Sir Hugh unclasped his arms. She went to her chair, sat down, leaned on the table, still covering her eyes. So she had leaned, years ago, with hidden face, in telling Bertram of the coming of the child. It seemed to her now that her shame was more complete, more overwhelming. And, though it overwhelmed her, her bliss was there; the golden and the black streams ran together.

"Dearest,—should I have been less sudden?" Sir Hugh was beside her, leaning over her, reasoning, questioning, only just not caressing her. "It's not as if we didn't know each other, Amabel: we have been strangers, in a sense;—yet, through it all—all these years—haven't we felt near?—Ah darling, you can't deny it;—you can't deny you love me." His arm was pressing her.

"Please—" she prayed again, and he moved his hand further away, beyond her crouching shoulder.

"You are such a little nun that you can't bear to be loved?—Is that it? But you'll have to learn again. You are more than a nun: you are a beautiful woman: young; wonderfully young. It's astonishing how like a girl you are."—Sir Hugh seemed to muse over a fact that allured. "And however like a nun you've lived — you can't deny that you love me."

"You haven't loved me," Amabel at last could say.

He paused, but only for a moment. "Perhaps not: but," his voice had now the delicate aptness that she remembered, "how could I believe that there was a chance for me? How could I think you could ever come to care, like this, when you had left me — you know — Amabel."

She was silent, her mind whirling. And his nearness, as he leaned over her, was less ecstasy than terror. It was as if she only knew her love, her sacred love again, when he was not near.

"It's quite of late that I've begun to wonder," said Sir Hugh. "Stupid ass of course, not to have seen the jewel I held in my hand. But you've only showed me the nun, you darling. I knew you cared, but I never knew how much. — I ought to have had more self-conceit, oughtn't I?"

"I have cared. You have been all that is beautiful. — I have cared more than for anything. — But — oh, it could not have been this. — This would have killed me with shame," said Amabel.

"With shame? Why, you strange angel?"

"Can you ask?" she said in a trembling voice.

His hand caressed her hair, slipped around her neck. "You nun; you saint. — Does that girlish peccadillo still haunt you?"

"Don't — oh don't — call it that — call me that! — "

"Call you a saint? But what else are you? — a beautiful saint. What other woman could have lived the life you've lived? It's wonderful."

"Don't. I cannot bear it."

"Can't bear to be called a saint? Ah, but, you see, that's just why you are one."

She could not speak. She could not even say the only answering word: a sinner. Her hands were like leaden weights upon her brows. In the darkness she heard her heart beating heavily, and tried and tried to catch some fragment of meaning from her whirling thoughts.

And as if her self-condemnation were a further enchantment, her husband murmured: "It makes you all the lovelier that you should feel like that. It makes me more in love with you than ever: but forget it now. Let me make you forget it. I can.—Darling, your beautiful hair. I remember it;—it is as beautiful as ever.—I remember it;—it fell to your knees.—Let me see your face, Amabel."

She was shuddering, shrinking from him.—"Oh—no—no.—Do you not see—not feel—that it is impossible—"

"Impossible! Why?—My darling, you are my wife;—and if you love me?—"

They were whirling impossibilities; she could see none clearly but one that flashed out for her now in her extremity of need, bright, ominous, accusing. She seized it:—"Augustine."

"Augustine? What of him?" Sir Hugh's voice had an edge to it.

"He could not bear it. It would break his heart."

"What has he to do with it? He isn't all your life:—you've given him most of it already."

"He is, he must be, all my life, except that beautiful part that you were:—that you are:—oh you will stay my friend!"—

"I'll stay your lover, your determined lover and husband, Amabel. Darling, you are ridiculous, enchanting—with your barriers, your scruples." The fear, the austerity, he felt in her fanned his ardour to flame. His arms once more went round her; he murmured words of lover-like pleading, rapturous, wild and foolish. And, though her love, her sacred love for him was there, his love for her was a nightmare to her now. She had lost herself, and it was as though she lost him, while he pleaded thus. And again and again she answered, resolute and tormented:—"No: no: never—never. Do not speak so to me.—Do not—I beg of you."

Suddenly he released her. He straightened himself, and moved away from her a little. Someone had entered.

Amabel dropped her hands and raised her eyes at last. Augustine stood before them.

Augustine had on still his long travelling coat; his cap, beaded with raindrops, was in his hand; his yellow hair was ruffled. He had entered hastily. He stood there looking at them, transfixed, yet not astonished. He was very pale.

For some moments no one of them spoke. Sir Hugh did not move further from his wife's side: he was neither anxious nor confused; but his face wore an involuntary scowl.

The deep confusion was Amabel's. But her husband had released her; no longer pleaded; and with the lifting of that dire oppression the realities of her life flooded her almost with relief. It was impossible, this gay, this facile, this unseemly love, but, as she rejected and put it from her, the old love was the stronger, cherished the more closely, in atonement and solicitude, the man shrunk from and repulsed. And in all the deep confusion, before her son,—that he should find her so, almost in her husband's arms,—a flash of clarity went through her mind as she saw them thus confronted. Deeper than ever between her and Augustine was the challenge of her love and his hatred; but it was that sacred love that now needed safeguards; she could not feel it when her husband was near and pleading; Augustine was her refuge from oppression.

She rose and went to him and timidly clasped his arm. "Dear Augustine, I am so glad you have come back. I have missed you so."

He stood still, not responding to her touch: but, as she held him, he looked across the room at Sir Hugh. "You wrote you missed me. That's why I came."

Sir Hugh now strolled to the fire and stood before it, turning to face Augustine's gaze; unperturbed; quite at ease.

"How wet you are dear," said Amabel. "Take off this coat."

Augustine stripped it off and flung it on a chair. She could hear his quick breathing: he did not look at her. And still it seemed to her that it was his anger rather than his love that protected her.

"He will want to change, dearest," said Sir Hugh from before the fire. "And,—I want to finish my talk with you."

Augustine now looked at his mother, at the blush that overwhelmed her as that possessive word was spoken. "Do you want me to go?"

"No, dear, no.—It is only the coat that is wet, isn't it. Don't go: I want to see you, of course, after your absence.—Hugh, you will excuse us; it seems such a long time since I saw him. You and I will finish our talk on another day.—Or I will write to you."

She knew what it must look like to her husband, this weak recourse to the protection of Augustine's presence; it looked like bashfulness, a further feminine wile, made up of self-deception and allurement, a putting off of final surrender for the greater sweetness of delay. And as the reading of him flashed through her it brought a strange pang of shame, for him; of regret, for something spoiled.

Sir Hugh took out his watch and looked at it. "Five o'clock. I told the station fly to come back for me at five fifteen. You'll give me some tea, dearest?"

"Of course;—it is time now.—Augustine, will you ring?"

The miserable blush covered her again.

The tea came and they were silent while the maid set it out. Augustine had thrown himself into a chair and stared before him. Sir Hugh, very much in possession, kept his place before the fire. Catching Amabel's eye he smiled at her. He was completely assured. How should he not be? What, for his seeing, could stand between them now?

When the maid was gone and Amabel was making tea, he came and stood over her, his hands in his pockets, his handsome head bent to her, talking lightly, slightly jesting, his voice pitched intimately for her ear, yet not so intimately that any unkindness of exclusion should appear. Augustine could hear all he said and gauge how deep was an intimacy that could wear such lightness, such slightness, as its mask.

Augustine, meanwhile, looked at neither his mother nor Sir Hugh. Turned from them in his chair he put out his hand for his tea and stared before him, as if unseeing and unhearing, while he drank it.

It was for her sake, Amabel knew, that Sir Hugh, raising his voice presently, as though aware of the sullen presence, made a little effort to lift the gloom. "What sort of a time have you had, Augustine?" he asked. "Was the weather at Haversham as bad as everywhere else?"

Augustine did not turn his head in replying:—"Quite as bad, I fancy."

"You and young Wallace hammered at metaphysics, I suppose."

"We did."

"Nice lad."

To this Augustine said nothing.

"They're such a solemn lot, the youths of this generation," said Sir Hugh, addressing Amabel as well as Augustine: "In my day we never bothered ourselves much about things: at least the ones I knew didn't. Awfully empty and frivolous. Augustine and his friends would have thought us. Where we used to talk about race horses they talk about the Absolute,—eh, Augustine? We used to go and hear comic-operas and they go and hear Brahms. I suppose you do go and hear Brahms, Augustine?"

Augustine maintained his silence as though not conceiving that the sportive question required an answer and Amabel said for him that he was very fond of Brahms.

"Well, I must be off," said Sir Hugh. "I hope your heart will ache ever so little for me, Amabel, when you think of the night you've turned me out into."

"Oh—but—I don't turn, you out,"—she stammered, rising, as, in a gay farewell, he looked at her.

"No? Well, I'm only teasing. I could hardly have managed to stay this time—though,—I might have managed, Amabel—. I'll come again soon, very soon," said Sir Hugh.

"No," her hand was in his and she knew that Augustine had turned his head and was looking at them:—"No, dear Hugh. Not soon, please. I will write." Sir Hugh looked at her smiling. He glanced at Augustine; then back at her, rallying her, affectionately, threateningly, determinedly, for her foolish feints. He raised her hand to his lips and kissed it. "Write, if you want to; but I'm coming," he said. He nodded to Augustine and left the room.

IX

I t was, curiously enough, a crippling awkwardness and embarrassment that Amabel felt rather than fear or antagonism, during that evening and the morning that followed. Augustine had left the room directly after Sir Hugh's departure. When she saw him again he showed her a face resolutely mute. It was impossible to speak to him; to explain. The main facts he must see; that her husband was making love to her and that, however deep her love for him, she rejected him.

Augustine might believe that rejection to be for his own sake, might believe that she renounced love and sacrificed herself from a maternal sense of duty; and, indeed, the impossibility of bringing that love into her life with Augustine had been the clear impossibility that had flashed for her in her need; she had seized upon it and it had armed her in her reiterated refusal. But how tell Augustine that there had been more than the clear impossibility; how tell him that deeper than renouncement was recoil? To tell that would be a disloyalty to her husband; it would be almost to accuse him; it would be to show Augustine that something in her life was spoiled and that her husband had spoiled it. So perplexed, so jaded, was she, so tossed by the conflicting currents of her lesser plight, that the deeper fears were forgotten: she was not conscious of being afraid of Augustine.

The rain had ceased next morning. The sky was crystalline; the wet earth glittered in Autumnal sunshine.

Augustine went out for his ride and Amabel had her girls to read with. There was a sense of peace for her in finding these threads of her life unknotted, smooth and simple, lying ready to her hand.

When she saw Augustine at lunch he said that he had met Lady Elliston.

"She was riding with Marjory and her girl."

"Oh, she is back, then." Amabel was grateful to him for his every-day tone.

"What is Lady Elliston's girl like?"

"Pretty; very; foolish manners I thought; Marjory looked bewilde-red by her."

"The manners of girls have changed, I fancy, since my day; and she isn't a boy-girl, like our nice Marjory, either?"

"No; she is a girl-girl; a pretty, forward, conceited girl-girl," said the ruthless Augustine. "Lady Elliston is coming to see you this afternoon; she asked me to tell you; she says she wants a long talk."

Amabel's weary heart sank at the news.

"She is coming soon after lunch," said Augustine.

"Oh—dear—"—. She could not conceal her dismay.

"But you knew that you were to see her again;—do you mind so much?" said Augustine.

"I don't mind.—It is only;—I have got so out of the way of seeing people that it is something of a strain."

"Would you like me to come in and interrupt your talk?" asked Augustine after a moment.

She looked across the table at him. Still, in her memory, preoccupied with the cruelty of his accusation, it was the anger rather than the love of his parting words the other day that was the more real. He had been hard in kindness, relentless in judgment, only not accusing her, not condemning her, because his condemnation had fixed on the innocent and not on the guilty—the horror of that, as well as the other horror, was between them now, and her guilt was deepened by it. But, as she looked, his eyes reminded her of something; was it of that fancied cry within the church, imprisoned and supplicating? They were like that cry of pain, those eyes, the dark rims of the iris strangely expanding, and her heart answered them, ignorant of what they said.

"You are thoughtful for me, dear; but no," she replied, "it isn't necessary for you to interrupt."

He looked away from her: "I don't know that it's not necessary," he said. After lunch they went into the garden and walked for a little in the sunlight, in almost perfect silence. Once or twice, as though from the very pressure of his absorption in her he created some intention of speech and fancied that her lips had parted with the words, Augustine turned his head quickly towards her, and at this, their eyes meeting, as it were over emptiness, both he and she would flush and look away again. The stress between them was painful. She was glad when he said that he had work to do and left her alone.

Amabel went to the drawing-room and took her chair near the table. A sense of solitude deeper than she had known for years pressed upon her. She closed her eyes and leaned back her head, thinking, dimly, that now, in such solitude as this, she must find her way to prayer again. But still the door was closed. It was as if she could not enter without a human hand in hers. Augustine's hand had never led her in; and she could not take her husband's now.

But her longing itself became almost a prayer as she sat with closed eyes. This would pass, this cloud of her husband's lesser love. When he knew her so unalterably firm, when he saw how inflexibly the old love shut out the new, he would, once more, be her friend. Then, feeling him near again, she might find peace. The thought of it was almost peace. Even in the midst of yesterday's bewildered pain she had caught glimpses of the old beauty; his kindly speech to Augustine, his making of ease for her; gratitude welled up in her and she sighed with the relief of her deep hope. To feel this gratitude was to see still further beyond the cloud. It was even beautiful for him to be able to "fall in love" with her—as he had put it: that the manifestations of his love should have made her shrink was not his fault but hers; she was a nun; because she had been a sinner. She almost smiled now, in seeing so clearly that it was on her the shadow rested. She could not be at peace, she could not pray, she could not live, it seemed to her, if he were really sha-dowed. And after the smile it was almost with the sense of dew falling upon her soul that she remembered the kindness, the chival-rous protection that had encompassed her through the long years. He was her friend, her knight; she would forget, and he, too, would forget that he had thought himself her lover.

She did not know how tired she was, but her exhaustion must have been great, for the thoughts faded into a vague sweetness, then were gone, and, suddenly opening her eyes, she knew that she had fallen asleep, sitting straightly in her chair, and that Lady Elliston was looking at her.

She started up, smiling and confused. "How absurd of me: — I have been sleeping. — Have you just come?"

Lady Elliston did not smile and was silent. She took Amabel's hand and looked at her; she had to recover herself from something; it may have been the sleeping face, wasted and innocent, that had touched her too deeply. And her gravity, as of repressed tears, frightened Amabel. She had never seen Lady Elliston look so grave. "Is anything the matter?" she asked. For a moment longer Lady Elliston was silent, as though reflecting. Then releasing Amabel's hand, she said: "Yes: I think something is the matter."

"You have come to tell me?"

"I didn't come for that. Sit down, Amabel. You are very tired, more tired than the other day. I have been looking at you for a long time. — I didn't come to tell you anything; but now, perhaps, I shall have something to tell. I must think."

She took a chair beside the table and leaned her head on her hand shading her eyes. Amabel had obeyed her and sat looking at her guest.

"Tell me," Lady Elliston said abruptly, and Amabel today, more than of sweetness and softness, was conscious of her strength, "have you been having a bad time since I saw you? Has anything happened? Has anything come between you and Augustine? I saw him this morning, and he's been suffering, too: I guessed it. You must be frank with me, Amabel; you must trust me: perhaps I am going to be franker with you, to trust you more, than you can dream."

She inspired the confidence her words laid claim to; for the first time in their lives Amabel trusted her unreservedly.

"I have had a very bad time," she said: "And Augustine has had a bad time. Yes; something has come between Augustine and me, — many things."

"He hates Hugh," said Lady Elliston.

"How can you know that?"

"I guessed it. He is a clever boy: he sees you absorbed; he sees your devotion robbing him; perhaps he sees even more, Amabel; I heard this morning, from Mrs. Grey, that Hugh had been with you, again, yesterday. Amabel, is it possible; has Hugh been making love to you?"

Amabel had become very pale. Looking down, she said in a hardly audible voice; "It is a mistake.—He will see that it is impossible."

Lady Elliston for a moment was silent: the confirming of her own suspicion seemed to have stupefied her. "Is it impossible?" she then asked.

"Quite, quite impossible."

"Does Hugh know that it is impossible?"

"He will.—Yesterday, Augustine came in while he was here;—I could not say any more."

"I see: I see"; said Lady Elliston. Her hand fell to the table now and she slightly tapped her finger-tips upon it. There was an ominous rhythm in the little raps. "And this adds to Augustine's hatred," she said.

"I am afraid it is true. I am afraid he does hate him, and how terrible that is," said Amabel, "for he believes him to be his father."

"By instinct he must feel the tie unreal."

"Yet he has had a father's kindness, almost, from Hugh."

"Almost. It isn't enough you know. He suspects nothing, you think?"

"It is that that is so terrible. He doesn't suspect me: he suspects him. He couldn't suspect evil of me. It is my guilt, and his ignorant hatred that is parting us." Amabel was trembling; she leaned forward and covered her face with her hands.

The very air about her seemed to tremble; so strange, so incredibly strange was it to hear her own words of helpless avowal; so strange to feel that she must tell Lady Elliston all she wished to know.

"Parting you? What do you mean? What folly! — what impossible folly! A mother and a son, loving each other as you and Augustine love, parted for that. Oh, no," said Lady Elliston, and her own voice shook a little: "that can't be. I won't have that."

"He would not love me, if he knew."

"Knew? What is there for him to know? And how should he know? You won't be so mad as to tell him?"

"It's my punishment not to dare to tell him — and to see my cowardice cast a shadow on Hugh."

"Punishment? haven't you been punished enough, good heavens! Cowardice? it is reason, maturity; the child has no right to your secret — it is yours and only yours, Amabel. And if he did know all, he could not judge you as you judge yourself."

"Ah, you don't understand," Amabel murmured: "I had forgotten to judge myself; I had forgotten my sin; it was Augustine who made me remember; I know now what he feels about people like me."

Again Lady Elliston controlled herself to a momentary silence and again her fingers sharply beat out her uncontrollable impatience. "I live in a world, Amabel," she said at last, "where people when they use the word 'sin,' in that connection, know that it's obsolete, a mere decorative symbol for unconventionality. In my world we don't have your cloistered black and white view of life nor see sin where only youth and trust and impulse were. If one takes risks, one may have to pay for them, of course; one plays the game, if one is in the ring, and, of course, you may be put out of the ring if you break the rules; but the rules are those of wisdom, not of morality, and the rule that heads the list is: Don't be found out. To imagine that the rules are anything more than matters of social convenience is to dignify the foolish game. It is a foolish game, Amabel, this of life: but one or two things in it are worth having; power to direct the game; freedom to break its rules; and love, passionate love, between a man and woman: and if one is strong enough one can have them all."

Lady Elliston had again put her hand to her brow, shielding her eyes and leaning her elbow on the table, and Amabel had raised her head and sat still, gazing at her.

"You weren't strong enough," Lady Elliston went on after a little pause: "You made frightful mistakes: the greatest, of course, was in running away with Paul Quentin: that was foolish, and it was, if you like to call foolishness by its obsolete name, a sin. You shouldn't have gone: you should have stayed: you should have kept your lover—as long as you wanted to."

Again she paused. "Do I horrify you?"

"No: you don't horrify me," Amabel replied. Her voice was gentle, almost musing; she was absorbed in her contemplation.

"You see," said Lady Elliston, "you didn't play the game: you made a mess of things and put the other players out. If you had stayed, and kept your lover, you would have been, in my eyes, a less loveable but a wiser woman. I believe in the game being kept up; I believe in the social structure: I am one of its accredited upholders"; in the shadow of her hand, Lady Elliston slightly smiled. "I believe in the family, the group of shared interests, shared responsibilities, shared opportunities it means: I don't care how many lovers a woman has if she doesn't break up the family, if she plays the game. Marriage is a social compact and it's the woman's part to keep the home together. If she seeks love outside marriage she must play fair, she mustn't be an embezzling partner; she mustn't give her husband another man's children to support and so take away from his own children;—that's thieving. The social structure, the family, are unharmed, if one is brave and wise. Love and marriage can rarely be combined and to renounce love is to cripple one's life, to miss the best thing it has to give. You, at all events, Amabel, may be glad that you haven't missed it. What, after all, does our life mean but just that,—the power and feeling that one gets into it. Be glad that you've had something."

Amabel, answering nothing, contemplated her guest.

"So, as these are my views, imagine what I feel when I find you here, like this"; Lady Elliston dropped her hand at last and looked about her, not at Amabel: "when I find you, in prison, locked up for life, by yourself, because you were lovably unwise. It's abominable, it's shameful, your position, isolated here, and tolerated, looked askance at by these nobodies. — Ah — I don't say that other women haven't paid even more heavily than you've done; I own that, to a certain extent, you've escaped the rigours that the game exacts from its victims. But there was no reason why you should pay anything: it wasn't known, never really known — your brother and Hugh saw to that; — you could have escaped scot-free."

Amabel spoke at last: "How, scot-free?" she asked.

Lady Elliston looked hard at her: "Your husband would have taken you back, had you insisted. — You shouldn't have fallen in with his plans."

"His plans? They were mine; my brother's."

"And his. Hugh was glad to be rid of the young wife he didn't love."

Again Amabel was trembling. "He might have been rid of her, altogether rid of her, if he had cared more for power and freedom than for pity."

"Power? With not nearly enough money? He was glad to keep her money and be rid of her. If you had pulled the purse-strings tight you might have made your own conditions."

"I do not believe you," said Amabel; "What you say is not true. My husband is noble."

Lady Elliston looked at her steadily and unflinchingly. "He is not noble," she said.

"What have you meant by coming here today? You have meant something! I will not listen to you! You are my husband's enemy;" — Amabel half started from her chair, but Lady Elliston laid her hand on her arm, looking at her so fixedly that she sank down again, panic-stricken.

"He is not noble," Lady Elliston repeated. "I will not have you waste your love as you have wasted your life. I will not have this illusion of his nobility come between you and your son. I will not have him come near you with his love. He is not noble, he is not generous, he is not beautiful. He could not have got rid of you. And he came to you with his love yesterday because his last mistress has thrown him over — and he must have a mistress. I know him: I know all about him: and you don't know him at all. Your husband was my lover for over twenty years."

A long silence followed her words. It was again a strange picture of arrested life in the dark room. The light fell quietly upon the two faces, their stillness, their contemplation — it seemed hardly more intent than contemplation, that drinking gaze of Amabel's; the draught of wonder was too deep for pain or passion, and Lady Elliston's eyes yielded, offered, held firm the cup the other drank. And the silence grew so long that it was as if the twenty years flowed by while they gazed upon each other.

It was Lady Elliston's face that first showed change. She might have been the cup-bearer tossing aside the emptied cup, seeing in the slow dilation of the victim's eyes, the constriction of lips and nostrils, that it had held poison. All — all had been drunk to the last drop. Death seemed to gaze from the dilated eyes.

"Oh — my poor Amabel — " Lady Elliston murmured; her face was stricken with pity.

Amabel spoke in the cramped voice of mortal anguish. — "Before he married me."

"Yes," Lady Elliston nodded, pitiful, but unflinching. "He married you for your money, and because you were a sweet, good, simple child who would not interfere."

"And he could not have divorced me, because of you."

"Because of me. You know the law; one guilty person can't divorce another. No one knew: no one has ever known: he and Jack have remained the best of friends: — but, of course, with all our care, it's been suspected, whispered. If I'd been less powerful the whispers might have blighted me: as it was, we thought that Bertram wasn't altogether unsuspecting. Hugh knew that it would be fatal to bring the matter into court; — I will say for Hugh that, in spite of the money, he wanted to. He could have married money again. He has always been extremely captivating. When he found that he would have to keep you, the money, of course, did atone. I suppose he has had most of your money by now," said Lady Elliston.

Amabel shut her eyes. "Wasn't he even sorry for me?" she asked.

Lady Elliston reflected and a glitter was in her eye; vengeance as well as justice armed her. "He is not unkind," she conceded: "and he was sorry after a fashion: 'Poor little girl,' I remember he said. Yes, he was very tolerant. But he didn't think of you at all, unless he wanted money. He is always graceful in his direct relations with people; he is tactful and sympathetic and likes things to be pleasant. But he doesn't mind breaking your heart if he doesn't have to see you while he is doing it. He is kind, but he is as hard as steel," said Lady Elliston.

"Then you do not love him any longer," said Amabel. It was not a question, only a farther acceptance.

And now, after only the slightest pause, Lady Elliston proved how deep, how unflinching was her courage. She had guarded her illicit passion all her life; she revealed it now. "I do love him," she said. "I have never loved another man. It is he who doesn't love me."

From the black depths where she seemed to swoon and float, like a drowsy, drowning thing, the hard note of misery struck on Amabel's ear. She opened her eyes and looked at Lady Elliston. Power, freedom, passion: it was not these that looked back at her from the bereft and haggard eyes. "After twenty years he has grown tired," Lady Elliston said; and her candour seemed as inevitable as Amabel's had been: each must tell the other everything; a common bond of suffering was between them and a common bond of love, though love so differing. "I knew, of course, that he was often unfaithful to me; he is a libertine; but I was the centre; he always came back to me. — I saw the end approaching about five years ago. I fought — oh how warily — so that he shouldn't dream I was afraid; — it is fatal for a woman to let a man know she is afraid, — the brutes, the cruel brutes," — said Lady Elliston; — "how we love them for their fear and pleading; how our fear and pleading hardens them against us." Her lips trembled and the tears ran down her cheeks. "I never pleaded; I never showed that I saw the change. I kept him, for years, by my skill. But the odds were too great at last. It was a year ago that he told me he didn't care any more. He was troubled, a little embarrassed, but quite determined that I shouldn't bother him. Since then it has been another woman. I know her; I meet her everywhere; very beautiful; very young; only married for three years; a heartless, rapacious creature. Hugh has nearly ruined himself in paying her jeweller's bills and her debts at bridge. And already she has thrown him over. It happened only the other day. I knew it was happening when I saw him here. I was glad, Amabel; I longed for him to suffer; and he will. He is a libertine of most fastidious tastes and he will not find many more young and beautiful women, of his world, to run risks for him. He, too, is getting old. And he has gone through nearly all his own money—and yours. Things will soon be over for him.—Oh—but—I love him—I love him—and everything is over for me.—How can I bear it!"

She bent forward on her knees and convulsive sobs shook her.

Her words seemed to Amabel to come to her from a far distance; they echoed in her, yet they were not the words she could have used. How dim was her own love-dream beside this torment of dispossession. What—who—had she loved for all these years? She could not touch or see her own grief; but Lady Elliston's grief pierced through her. She leaned towards her and softly touched her shoulder, her arm, her hand; she held the hand in hers. The sight of this loss of strength and dignity was an actual pain; her own pain was something elusive and unsubstantial; it wandered like a ghost vainly seeking an embodiment.

"Oh, you angel—you poor angel!" moaned Lady Elliston. "There: that's enough of crying; it can't bring back my youth.—What a fool I am. If only I could learn to think of myself as free instead of maimed and left by the wayside. It is hard to live without love if one has always had it.—But I have freed you, Amabel. I am glad of that. It has been a cruel, but a right thing to do. He shall not come to you with his shameless love; he shall not come between you and your boy. You shan't misplace your worship so. It is Augustine who is beautiful and noble; it is Augustine who loves you. You aren't maimed and forsaken; thank heaven for that, dear."

Lady Elliston had risen. Strong again, she faced her life, took up the reins, not a trace of scruple or of shame about her. It did not enter her mind to ask Amabel for forgiveness, to ask if she were despised or shrunk from: it did not enter Amabel's mind to wonder at the omission. She looked up at her guest and her lifted face seemed that of the drowned creature floating to the surface of the water.

"Tell me, Amabel," Lady Elliston suddenly pleaded, "this is not going to blacken things for you; you won't let it blacken things. You will live; you will leave your prison and come out into the world, with your splendid boy, and live."

Amabel slightly shook her head.

"Oh, why do you say that? Has it hurt so horribly?"

Amabel seemed to make the effort to think what it had done. She did not know. The ghost wailed; but she could not see its form.

"Did you care—so tremendously—about him?"—Lady Elliston asked, and her voice trembled. And, for answer, the drowned eyes looked up at her through strange, cold tears.

"Oh, my dear, my dear," Lady Elliston murmured. Her hand was still in Amabel's and she stood there beside her, her hand so held, for a long, silent moment. They had looked away from each other.

And in the silence each knew that it was the end and that they would see each other no more. They lived in different planets, under different laws; they could understand, they could trust; but a deep, transparent chasm, like that of the ether flowing between two divided worlds, made them immeasurably apart.

Yet, when she at last gently released Amabel's hand, drawing her own away. Lady Elliston said: "But,—won't you come out now?"

"Out? Where?" Amabel asked, in the voice of that far distance.

"Into the world, the great, splendid world."

"Splendid?"

"Splendid, if you choose to seize it and take what it has to give."

After a moment Amabel asked: "Has it given you so much?"

Lady Elliston looked at her from across the chasm; it was not dark, it held no precipices; it was made up only of distance. Lady Elliston saw; but she was loyal to her own world. "Yes, it has," she said. "I've lived; you have dreamed your life away. You haven't even a reality to mourn the loss of."

"No," Amabel said; she closed her eyes and turned her head away against the chair; "No; I have lived too. Don't pity me."

X

I t was past five when Augustine came into the empty drawing-room. Tea was standing waiting, and had been there, he saw, for some time. He rang and asked the maid to tell Lady Channice. Lady Channice, he heard, was lying down and wanted no tea. Lady Elliston had gone half an hour before. After a moment or two of deliberation, Augustine sat down and made tea for himself. That was soon over. He ate nothing, looking with a vague gaze of repudiation at the plate of bread and butter and the cooling scones.

When tea had been taken away he walked up and down the room quickly, pausing now and then for further deliberation. But he decided that he would not go up to his mother. He went on walking for a long time. Then he took a book and read until the dressing-bell for dinner rang.

When he went upstairs to dress he paused outside his mother's door, as she had paused outside his, and listened. He heard no sound. He stood still there for some moments before lightly rapping on the door. "Who is it?" came his mother's voice. "I; Augustine. How are you? You are coming down?"

"Not tonight," she answered; "I have a very bad headache."

"But let me have something sent up." After a moment his mother's voice said very sweetly; "Of course, dear." And she added "I shall be all right tomorrow."

The voice sounded natural—yet not quite natural; too natural, perhaps, Augustine reflected. Its tone remained with him as something disturbing and prolonged itself in memory like a familiar note strung to a queer, forced pitch, that vibrated on and on until it hurt.

After his solitary meal he took up his book again in the drawing-room. He read with effort and concentration, his brows knotted; his young face, thus controlled to stern attention, was at once vigilant for outer impressions and absorbed in the inner interest. Once or twice he looked up, as a coal fell with a soft crash from the fire, as a thin creeper tapped sharply on the window pane. His mother's room was above the drawing-room and while he read he was listening; but he heard no footsteps.

Suddenly, dim, yet clear, came another sound, a sound familiar, though so rare; wheels grinding on the gravel drive at the other side of the house. Then, loud and startling at that unaccustomed hour, the old hall bell clanged through the house.

Augustine found himself leaning forward, breathing quickly, his book half-closed. At first he did not know what he was listening for or why his body should be tingling with excitement and anger. He knew a moment later. There was a step in the hall, a voice. All his life Augustine had known them, had waited for them, had hated them. Sir Hugh was back again.

Of course he was back again, soon,—as he had promised in the tone of mastery. But his mother had told him not to come; she had told him not to come, and in a tone that meant more than his. Did he not know?—Did he not understand?

"No, dear Hugh, not soon.—I will write."—Augustine sprang to his feet as he entered the room.

Sir Hugh had been told that he would not find his wife. His face wore its usual look of good-temper, but it wore more than its usual look of indifference for his wife's son. "Ah, tell Lady Channice, will you," he said over his shoulder to the maid. "How d'ye do, Augustine:" and, as usual, he strolled up to the fire.

Augustine watched him as he crossed the room and said nothing. The maid had closed the door. From his wonted place Sir Hugh surveyed the young man and Augustine surveyed him.

"You know, my dear fellow," said Sir Hugh presently, lifting the sole of his boot to the fire, "you've got devilish bad manners. You are devilishly impertinent, I may tell you."

Augustine received the reproof without comment.

"You seem to imagine," Sir Hugh went on, "that you have some particular right to bad manners and impertinence here, in this house; but you're mistaken; I belong here as well as you do; and you'll have to accept the fact."

A convulsive trembling, like his mother's, passed over the young man's face; but whereas only Amabel's hands and body trembled, it was the muscles of Augustine's lips, nostrils and brows that were affected, and to see the strength of his face so shaken was disconcerting, painful.

"You don't belong here while I'm here," he said, jerking the words out suddenly. "This is my mother's home—and mine;—but as soon as you make it insufferable for us we can leave it."

"*You* can; that's quite true," Sir Hugh nodded.

Augustine stood clenching his hands on his book. Now, unconscious of what he did, he grasped the leaves and wrenched them back and forth as he stood silent, helpless, desperate, before the other's intimation. Sir Hugh watched the unconscious violence with interest.

"Yes," he went on presently, and still with good temper; "if you make yourself insufferable—to your mother and me—you can go. Not that I want to turn you out. It rests with you. Only, you must see that you behave. I won't have you making her wretched."

Augustine glanced dangerously at him.

"Your mother and I have come to an understanding—after a great many years of misunderstanding," said Sir Hugh, putting up the other sole. "I'm—very fond of your mother,—and she is,—very fond of me."

"She doesn't know you," said Augustine, who had become livid while the other made his gracefully hesitant statement.

"Doesn't know me?" Sir Hugh lifted his brows in amused inquiry; "My dear boy, what do you know about that, pray? You are not in all your mother's secrets."

Augustine was again silent for a moment, and he strove for self-mastery. "If I am not in my mother's secrets," he said, "she is not in yours. She does not know you. She doesn't know what sort of a man you are. You have deceived her. You have made her think that you are reformed and that the things in your life that made her leave you won't come again. But whether you are reformed or not a man like you has no right to come near a woman like my mother. I know that you are an evil man," said Augustine, his face trembling more and more uncontrollably; "And my mother is a saint."

Sir Hugh stared at him. Then he burst into a shout of laughter. "You young fool!" he said.

Augustine's eyes were lightnings in a storm-swept sky.

"You young fool," Sir Hugh repeated, not laughing, a heavier stress weighting each repeated word.

"Can you deny," said Augustine, "that you have always led a dissolute life? If you do deny it it won't help you. I know it: and I've not needed the echoes to tell me. I've always felt it in you. I've always known you were evil."

"What if I don't deny it?" Sir Hugh inquired.

Augustine was silent, biting his quivering lips.

"What if I don't deny it?" Sir Hugh repeated. His assumption of good-humour was gone. He, too, was scowling now. "What have you to say then?"

"By heaven,—I say that you shall not come near my mother."

"And what if it was not because of my dissolute life she left me? What if you've built up a cock-and-bull romance that has no relation to reality in your empty young head? What then? Ask your mother if she left me because of my dissolute life," said Sir Hugh.

The book in Augustine's wrenching hands had come apart with a crack and crash. He looked down at it stupidly.

"You really should learn to control yourself—in every direction, my dear boy," Sir Hugh remarked. "Now, unless you would like to wreak your temper on the furniture, I think you had better sit down and be still. I should advise you to think over the fact that saints have been known before now to forgive sinners. And sinners may not be so bad as your innocence imagines. Goodbye. I am going up to see your mother. I am going to spend the night here."

Augustine stood holding the shattered book. He gazed as stupidly at Sir Hugh as he had gazed at it. He gazed while Sir Hugh, who kept a rather wary eye fixed on him, left the fire and proceeded with a leisurely pace to cross the room: the door was reached and the handle turned, before the stupor broke. Sir Hugh, his eyes still fixed on his antagonist, saw the blanched fury, the start, as if the dazed body were awakening to some insufferable torture, saw the gathering together, the leap:—"You fool—you young fool!" he ground between his teeth as, with a clash of the half-opened door, Augustine pinned him upon it. "Let me go. Do you hear. Let me go." His voice was the voice of the lion-tamer, hushed before danger to a quelling depth of quiet.

And like the young lion, drawing long breaths through dilated-nostrils, Augustine growled back:—"I will not—I will not.—You shall not go to her. I would rather kill you."

"Kill me?" Sir Hugh smiled. "It would be a fight first, you know."

"Then let it be a fight. You shall not go to her."

"And what if she wants me to go to her.—Will you kill her first, too—"—The words broke. Augustine's hand was on his throat. Sir Hugh seized him. They writhed together against the door. "You mad-man!—You damned mad-man!—Your mother is in love with me.—I'll put you out of her life—"—Sir Hugh grated forth from the strangling clutch.

Suddenly, as they writhed, panting, glaring their hatred at each other, the door they leaned on pushed against them. Someone outside was turning the handle, was forcing it open. And, as if through the shocks and flashes of a blinding, deafening tempest, Augustine heard his mother's voice, very still, saying: "Let me come in."

XI

T hey fell apart and moved back into the room. Amabel entered. She wore a long white dressing-gown that, to her son's eyes, made her more than ever look her sainted self; she had dressed hastily, and, on hearing the crash below, she had wrapped a white scarf about her head and shoulders, covering her unbound hair. So framed and narrowed her face was that of a shrouded corpse: the same strange patience stamped it; her eyes, only, seemed to live, and they, too, were patient and ready for any doom.

Quietly she had closed the door, and standing near it now she looked at them; her eyes fell for a moment upon Sir Hugh; then they rested on Augustine and did not leave him.

Sir Hugh spoke first. He laughed a little, adjusting his collar and tie.

"My dear,—you've saved my life. Augustine was going to batter my brains out on the door, I fancy."

She did not look at him, but at Augustine.

"He's really dangerous, your son, you know. Please don't leave me alone with him again," Sir Hugh smiled and pleaded; it was with almost his own lightness, but his face still twitched with anger.

"What have you said to him?" Amabel asked.

Augustine's eyes were drawing her down into their torment.— Unfortunate one.—That presage of her maternity echoed in her now. His stern young face seemed to have been framed, destined from the first for this foreseen misery.

Sir Hugh had pulled himself together. He looked at the mother and son. And he understood her fear.

He went to her, leaned over her, a hand above her shoulder on the door. He reassured and protected her; and, truly, in all their story, it had never been with such sincerity and grace.

"Dearest, it's nothing. I've merely had to defend my rights. Will you assure this young firebrand that my misdemeanours didn't force you to leave me. That there were misdemeanours I don't deny; and of course you are too good for the likes of me; but your coming away wasn't my fault, was it.—That's what I've said.—And that saints forgive sinners, sometimes.—That's all I want you to tell him."

Amabel still gazed into her son's eyes. It seemed to her, now that she must shut herself out from it for ever, that for the first time in all her life she saw his love.

It broke over her; it threatened and commanded her; it implored and supplicated—ah the supplication beyond words or tears!—

Selflessness made it stern. It was for her it threatened; for her it prayed.

All these years the true treasure had been there beside her, while she worshipped at the spurious shrine. Only her sorrow, her solicitude had gone out to her son; the answering love that should have cherished and encompassed him flowed towards its true goal only when it was too late. He could not love her when he knew.

And he was to know. That had come to her clearly and unalterably while she had leaned, half fallen, half kneeling, against her bed, dying, it seemed to her, to all that she had known of life or hope.

But all was not death within her. In the long, the deadly stupor, her power to love still lived. It had been thrown back from its deep channel and, wave upon wave, it seemed heaped upon itself in some narrow abyss, tormented and shuddering; and at last by its own strength, rather than by thought or prayer of hers, it had forced an outlet.

It was then as if she found herself once more within the church. Darkness, utter darkness was about her; but she was prostrated before the unseen altar. She knew herself once more, and with herself she knew her power to love.

Her life and all its illusions passed before her; by the truth that irradiated the illusions, she judged them and herself and saw what must be the atonement. All that she had believed to be the treasure of her life had been taken from her; but there was one thing left to her that she could give:—her truth to her son. When that price was paid, he would be hers to love; he was no longer hers to live for. He should found his life on no illusions, as she had founded hers. She must set him free to turn away from her; but when he turned away it would not be to leave her in the loneliness and the terror of heart that she had known; it would be to leave her in the church where she could pray for him.

She answered her husband after her long silence, looking at her son.

"It is true, Augustine," she said. "You have been mistaken. I did not leave him for that."

Sir Hugh drew a breath of satisfaction. He glanced round at Augustine. It was not a venomous glance, but, with its dart of steely intention, it paid a debt of vengeance. "So,—we needn't say anything more about it," he said. "And—dearest—perhaps now you'll tell Augustine that he may go and leave us together."

Amabel left her husband's side and went to her chair near the table. A strange calmness breathed from her. She sat with folded hands and downcast eyes.

"Augustine, come here," she said.

The young man came and stood before her.

"Give me your hand."

He gave it to her. She did not look at him but kept her eyes fixed on the ground while she clasped it.

"Augustine," she said, "I want you to leave me with my husband. I must talk with him. He is going away soon. Tomorrow— tomorrow morning early, I will see you, here. I will have a great deal to say to you, my dear son."

But Augustine, clutching her hand and trembling, looked down at her so that she raised her eyes to his.

"I can't go, till you say something, now, Mother;"—his voice shook as it had shaken on that day of their parting, his face was livid and convulsed, as then;—"I will go away tonight—I don't know that I can ever return—unless you tell me that you are not going to take him back." He gazed down into his mother's eyes.

She did not answer him; she did not speak. But, as he looked into them, he, too, for the first time, saw in them what she had seen in his.

They dwelt on him; they widened; they almost smiled; they deeply promised him all—all—that he most longed for. She was his, her son's; she was not her husband's. What he had feared had never threatened him or her. This was a gift she had won the right to give. The depth of her repudiation yesterday gave her her warrant.

And to Amabel, while they looked into each other's eyes, it was as if, in the darkness, some arching loveliness of dawn vaguely shaped itself above the altar.

"Kiss me, dear Augustine," she said. She held up her forehead, closing her eyes, for the kiss that was her own.

Augustine was gone. And now, before her, was the ugly breaking. But must it be so ugly? Opening her eyes, she looked at her husband as he stood before the fire, his wondering eyes upon her. Must it be ugly? Why could it not be quiet and even kind?

Strangely there had gathered in her, during the long hours, the garnered strength of her life of discipline and submission. It had sustained her through the shudder that glanced back at yesterday — at the corruption that had come so near; it had given sanity to see with eyes of compassion the forsaken woman who had come with her courageous, revengeful story; it gave sanity now, as she looked over at her husband, to see him also, with those eyes of compassionate understanding; he was not blackened, to her vision, by the shadowing corruption, but, in his way, pitiful, too; all the worth of life lost to him.

And it seemed swiftest, simplest, and kindest, as she looked over at him, to say: — "You see — Lady Elliston came this afternoon, and told me everything."

Sir Hugh kept his face remarkably unmoved. He continued to gaze at his wife with an unabashed, unstartled steadiness. "I might have guessed that," he said after a short silence. "Confound her."

Amabel made no reply.

"So I suppose," Sir Hugh went on, "you feel you can't forgive me."

She hesitated, not quite understanding. "You mean — for having married me — when you loved her?"

"Well, yes; but more for not having, long ago, in all these years, found out that you were the woman that any man with eyes to see, any man not blinded and fatuous, ought to have been in love with from the beginning."

Amabel flushed. Her vision was untroubled; but the shadow hovered. She was ashamed for him.

"No"; she said, "I did not think of that. I don't know that I have anything to forgive you. It is Lady Elliston, I think, who must try and forgive you, if she can."

Sir Hugh was again silent for a moment; then he laughed. "You dear innocent! — Well — I won't defend myself at her expense."

"Don't," said Amabel, looking now away from him.

Sir Hugh eyed her and seemed to weigh the meaning of her voice.

He crossed the room suddenly and leaned over her: — "Amabel darling, — what must I do to atone? I'll be patient. Don't be cruel and punish me for too long a time."

"Sit there — will you please." She pointed to the chair at the other side of the table.

He hesitated, still leaning above her; then obeyed; folding his arms; frowning.

"You don't understand," said Amabel. "I loved you for what you never were. I do not love you now. And I would never have loved you as you asked me to do yesterday."

He gazed at her, trying to read the difficult riddle of a woman's perversity. "You were in love with me yesterday," he said at last.

She answered nothing.

"I'll make you love me again."

"No: never," she answered, looking quietly at him. "What is there in you to love?"

Sir Hugh flushed. "I say! You are hard on me!"

"I see nothing loveable in you," said Amabel with her inflexible gentleness. "I loved you because I thought you noble and magnanimous; but you were neither. You only did not cast me off, as I deserved, because you could not; and you were kind partly because you are kind by nature, but partly because my money was convenient to you. I do not say that you were ignoble; you were in a very false position. And I had wronged you; I had committed the greater social crime; but there was nothing noble; you must see that; and it was for that I loved you."

Sir Hugh now got up and paced up and down near her.

"So you are going to cast me off because I had no opportunity for showing nobility. How do you know I couldn't have behaved as you believed I did behave, if only I'd had the chance? You know—you are hard on me."

"I see no sign of nobility—towards anyone—in your life," Amabel answered as dispassionately as before.

Sir Hugh walked up and down.

"I did feel like a brute about the money sometimes," he remarked;—"especially that last time; I wanted you to have the house as a sort of salve to my conscience; I've taken almost all your money, you know; it's quite true. As to the rest—what Augustine calls my dissoluteness—I can't pretend to take your view; a nun's view." He looked at her. "How beautiful you are with that white round your face," he said. "You are like a woman of snow."

She looked back at him as though, from the unhesitating steadiness of her gaze, to lend him some of her own clearness.

"Don't you see that it's not real? Don't you see that it's because you suddenly find me beautiful, and because, as a woman of snow, I allure you, that you think you love me? Do you really deceive yourself?"

He stared at her; but the ray only illumined the bewilderment of his dispossession. "I don't pretend to be an idealist," he said, stopping still before her; "I don't pretend that it's not because I suddenly find you beautiful; that's one reason; and a very essential one, I think; but there are other reasons, lots of them. Amabel—you must see that my love for you is an entirely different sort of thing from what my love for her ever was."

She said nothing. She could not argue with him, nor ask, as if for a cheap triumph, if it were different from his love for the later mistress. She saw, indeed, that it was different now, whatever it had been yesterday. Clearly she saw, glancing at herself as at an object in the drama, that she offered quite other interests and charms, that her attractions, indeed, might be of a quality to elicit quite new sentiments from Sir Hugh, sentiments less shadowing than those of yesterday had been. And so she accepted his interpretation in silence, unmoved by it though doing it full justice, and for a little while Sir Hugh said nothing either. He still stood before her and she no longer looked at him, but down at her folded hands that did not tremble at all tonight, and she wondered if now, perhaps, he would understand her silence and leave her. But when, in an altered voice, he said: "Amabel;" she looked at him.

She seemed to see everything tonight as a disembodied spirit might see it, aware of what the impeding flesh could only dimly manifest; and she saw now that her husband's face had never been so near beauty.

It did not attain it; it was, rather, as if the shadow, lifting entirely for a flickering moment, revealed something unconscious, something almost innocent, almost pitiful: it was as if, liberated, he saw beauty for a moment and put out his hands to it, like a child putting out its hands to touch the moon, believing that it was as near to him, and as easily to be attained, as pleasure always had been.

"Try to forgive me," he said, and his voice had the broken note of a sad child's voice, the note of ultimate appeal from man to woman. "I'm a poor creature; I know that. It's always made me ashamed—to see how you idealise me.—The other day, you know,—when you kissed my hand—I was horribly ashamed.—But, upon my honour Amabel, I'm not a bad fellow at bottom,—not the devil incarnate your son seems to think me. Something could be made of me, you know;—and, if you'll forgive me, and let me try to win your love again;—ah Amabel—"—he pleaded, almost with tears, before her unchangingly gentle face. And, the longing to touch her, hold her, receive comfort and love, mingling with the new reverential fear, he knelt beside her, putting his head on her knees and murmuring: "I do so desperately love you."

Amabel sat looking down upon him. Her face was unchanged, but in her heart was a trembling of astonished sadness.

It was too late. It had been too late—from the very first;—yet, if they could have met before each was spoiled for each;—before life had set them unalterably apart—? The great love of her life was perhaps not all illusion.

And she seemed to sit for a moment in the dark church, dreaming of the distant Spring-time, of brooks and primroses and prophetic birds, and of love, young, untried and beautiful. But she did not lay her hand on Sir Hugh's head nor move at all towards him. She sat quite still, looking down at him, like a Madonna above a passionate supplicant, pitiful but serene.

And as he knelt, with his face hidden, and did not hear her voice nor feel her touch, with an unaccustomed awe the realisation of her remoteness from him stole upon Sir Hugh.

Passion faded from his heart, even self-pity and longing faded. He entered her visionary retrospect and knew, like her, that it was too late; that everything was too late; that everything was really over. And, as he realised it, a chill went over him. He felt like a strayed reveller waking suddenly from long slumber and finding himself alone in darkness.

He lifted his face and looked at her, needing the reassurance of her human eyes; and they met his with their remote gentleness. For a long moment they gazed at each other.

Then Sir Hugh, stumbling a little, got upon his feet and stood, half turned from her, looking away into the room.

When he spoke it was in quite a different voice, it was almost the old, usual voice, the familiar voice of their friendly encounters.

"And what are you going to do with yourself, now, Amabel?"

"I am going to tell Augustine," she said.

"Tell him!" Sir Hugh looked round at her. "Why?"

"I must."

He seemed, after a long silence, to accept her sense of necessity as sufficient reason. "Will it cut him up very much, do you think?" he asked.

"It will change everything very much, I think," said Amabel.

"Do you mean — that he will blame you? — "

"I don't think that he can love me any longer."

There was no hint of self-pity in her calm tones and Sir Hugh could only formulate his resentment and his protest—and they were bitter,—by a muttered—"Oh—I say!—I say!—"

He went on presently; "And will you go on living here, perhaps alone?"

"Alone, I think; yes, I shall live here; I do not find it dismal, you know."

Sir Hugh felt himself again looking reluctantly into darkness. "But—how will you manage it, Amabel?" he asked.

And her voice seemed to come, in all serenity, from the darkness; "I shall manage it."

Yes, the awe hovered near him as he realised that what, to him, meant darkness, to her meant life. She would manage it. She had managed to live through everything.

A painful analogy came to increase his sadness;—it was like having before one a martyr who had been bound to rack after rack and still maintained that strange air of keeping something it was worth while being racked for. Glancing at her it seemed to him, still more painfully, that in spite of her beauty she was very like a martyr; that queer touch of wildness in her eyes; they were serene, they were even sweet, yet they seemed to have looked on horrid torments; and those white wrappings might have concealed dreadful scars.

He took out his watch, nervously and automatically, and looked at it. He would have to walk to the station; he could catch a train.

"And may I come, sometimes, and see you?" he asked. "I'll not bother you, you know. I understand, at last. I see what a blunder— an ugly blunder—this has been on my part. But perhaps you'll let me be your friend—more really your friend than I have ever been."

And now, as he glanced at her again, he saw that the gentleness was remote no longer. It had come near like a light that, in approaching, diffused itself and made a sudden comfort and sweetness. She was too weary to smile, but her eyes, dwelling gently on him, promised him something, as, when they had dwelt with their passion of exiled love on her son, they had promised something to Augustine. She held out her hand. "We are friends," she said.

Sir Hugh flushed darkly. He stood holding her hand, looking at it and not at her. He could not tell what were the confused emotions that struggled within him; shame and changed love; awe, and broken memories of prayers that called down blessings. It was "God bless you," that he felt, yet he did not feel that it was for him to say these words to her. And no words came; but tears were in his eyes as, in farewell, he bent over her hand and kissed it.

XII

W hen Amabel waked next morning a bright dawn filled her room. She remembered, finding it so light, that before lying down to sleep she had drawn all her curtains so that, through the open windows, she might see, until she fell asleep, a wonderful sky of stars. She had not looked at them for long. She had gone to sleep quickly and quietly, lying on her side, her face turned to the sky, her arms cast out before her, just as she had first lain down; and so she found herself lying when she waked.

It was very early. The sun gilded the dark summits of the sycamores that she could see from her window. The sky was very high and clear, and long, thin strips of cloud curved in lessening bars across it. The confused chirpings of the waking birds filled the air. And before any thought had come to her she smiled as she lay there, looking at and listening to the wakening life.

Then the remembrance of the dark ordeal that lay before her came. It was like waking to the morning that was to see one on the scaffold: but, with something of the light detachment that a condemned prisoner might feel — nothing being left to hope for and the only strength demanded being the passive strength to endure — she found that she was thinking more of the sky and of the birds than of the ordeal. Some hours lay between her and that; bright, beautiful hours.

She put out her hand and took her watch which lay near. Only six. Augustine would not expect to see her until ten. Four long hours: she must get up and spend them out of doors.

It was too early for hot water or maids; she enjoyed the flowing shocks of the cold and her own rapidity and skill in dressing and coiling up her hair. She put on her black dress and took her black scarf as a covering for her head. Slipping out noiselessly, like a truant school-girl, she made her way to the pantry, found milk and bread, and ate and drank standing, then, cautiously pushing bolts and bars, stepped from the door into the dew, the sunlight, the keen young air.

She took the path to the left that led through the sycamore wood, and crossing the narrow brook by a little plank and hand rail, passed into the meadows where, in Spring, she and Augustine used to pick cowslips.

She thought of Augustine, but only in that distant past, as a little child, and her mind dwelt on sweet, trivial memories, on the toys he had played with and the pair of baby-shoes, bright red shoes, square-toed, with rosettes on them, that she had loved to see him wear with his little white frocks. And in remembering the shoes she smiled again, as she had smiled in hearing the noisy chirpings of the waking birds.

The little path ran on through meadow after meadow, stiles at the hedges, planks over the brooks and ditches that intersected this flat, pastoral country. She paused for a long time to watch the birds hopping and fluttering in a line of sapling willows that bordered one of these brooks and at another stood and watched a water-rat, unconscious of her nearness, making his morning toilette on the bank; he rubbed his ears and muzzle hastily, with the most amusing gesture. Once she left the path to go close to some cows that were grazing peacefully; their beautiful eyes, reflecting the green pastures, looked up at her with serenity, and she delighted in the fragrance that exhaled from their broad, wet nostrils.

"Darlings," she found herself saying.

She went very far. She crossed the road that, seen from Charlock House, was, with its bordering elm-trees, only a line of blotted blue. And all the time the light grew more splendid and the sun rose higher in the vast dome of the sky.

She returned more slowly than she had gone. It was like a dream this walk, as though her spirit, awake, alive to sight and sound, smiling and childish, were out under the sky, while in the dark, sad house the heavily throbbing heart waited for its return.

This waiting heart seemed to come out to meet her as once more she saw the sycamores dark on the sky and saw beyond them the low stone house. The pearly, the crystalline interlude, drew to a close. She knew that in passing from it she passed into deep, accepted tragedy.

The sycamores had grown so tall since she first came to live at Charlock House that the foliage made a high roof and only sparkling chinks of sky showed through. The path before her was like the narrow aisle of a cathedral. It was very dark and silent.

She stood still, remembering the day when, after her husband's first visit to her, she had come here in the late afternoon and had known the mingled revelation of divine and human holiness. She stood still, thinking of it, and wondered intently, looking down.

It was gone, that radiant human image, gone for ever. The son, to whom her heart now clung, was stern. She was alone. Every prop, every symbol of the divine love had been taken from her. But, so bereft, it was not, after the long pause of wonder, in weakness and abandonment that she stood still in the darkness and closed her eyes.

It was suffering, but it was not fear; it was longing, but it was not loneliness. And as, in her wrecked girlhood, she had held out her hands, blessed and receiving, she held them out now, blessed, though sacrificing all she had. But her uplifted face, white and rapt, was now without a smile.

Suddenly she knew that someone was near her.

She opened her eyes and saw Augustine standing at some little distance looking at her. It seemed natural to see him there, waiting to lead her into the ordeal. She went towards him at once.

"Is it time?" she said. "Am I late?"

Augustine was looking intently at her. "It isn't half-past nine yet," he said. "I've had my breakfast. I didn't know you had gone out till just now when I went to your room and found it empty."

She saw then in his eyes that he had been frightened. He took her hand and she yielded it to him and they went up towards the house.

"I have had such a long walk," she said. "Isn't it a beautiful morning."

"Yes; I suppose so," said Augustine. As they walked he did not take his eyes off his mother's face.

"Aren't you tired?" he asked.

"Not at all. I slept well."

"Your shoes are quite wet," said Augustine, looking down at them.

"Yes; the meadows were thick with dew."

"You didn't keep to the path?"

"Yes;—no, I remember."—she looked down at her shoes, trying, obediently, to satisfy him, "I turned aside to look at the cows."

"Will you please change your shoes at once?"

"I'll go up now and change them. And will you wait for me in the drawing-room, Augustine."

"Yes." She saw that he was still frightened, and remembering how strange she must have looked to him, standing still, with upturned face and outstretched hands, in the sycamore wood, she smiled at him:—"I am well, dear, don't be troubled," she said.

In her room, before she went downstairs, she looked at herself in the glass. The pale, calm face was strange to her, or was it the story, now on her lips, that was the strange thing, looking at that face. She saw them both with Augustine's eyes; how could he believe it of that face. She did not see the mirrored holiness, but the innocent eyes looked back at her marvelling at what she was to tell of them.

In the drawing-room Augustine was walking up and down. The fire was burning cheerfully and all the windows were wide open. The room looked its lightest. Augustine's intent eyes were on her as she entered. "You won't find the air too much?" he questioned; his voice trembled.

She murmured that she liked it. But the agitation that she saw controlled in him affected her so that she, too, began to tremble.

She went to her chair at one side of the large round table. "Will you sit there, Augustine," she said.

He sat down, opposite to her, where Sir Hugh had sat the night before. Amabel put her elbows on the table and covered her face with her hands. She could not look at her child; she could not see his pain.

"Augustine," she said, "I am going to tell you a long story; it is about myself, and about you. And you will be brave, for my sake, and try to help me to tell it as quickly as I can."

His silence promised what she asked.

"Before the story," she said, "I will tell you the central thing, the thing you must be brave to hear.—You are an illegitimate child, Augustine." At that she stopped. She listened and heard nothing. Then came long breaths.

She opened her eyes to see that his head had fallen forward and was buried in his arms. "I can't bear it.—I can't bear it—" came in gasps.

She could say nothing. She had no word of alleviation for his agony. Only she felt it turning like a sword in her heart.

"Say something to me"—Augustine gasped on.—"You did that for him, too.—I am his child.—You are not my mother.—" He could not sob.

Amabel gazed at him. With the unimaginable revelation of his love came the unimaginable turning of the sword; it was this that she must destroy. She commanded herself to inflict, swiftly, the further blow.

"Augustine," she said.

He lifted a blind face, hearing her voice. He opened his eyes. They looked at each other.

"I am your mother," said Amabel.

He gazed at her. He gazed and gazed; and she offered herself to the crucifixion of his transfixing eyes.

The silence grew long. It had done its work. Once more she put her hands before her face. "Listen," she said. "I will tell you."

He did not stir nor move his eyes from her hidden face while she spoke. Swiftly, clearly, monotonously, she told him all. She paused at nothing; she slurred nothing. She read him the story of the stupid sinner from the long closed book of the past. There was no hesitation for a word; no uncertainty for an interpretation. Everything was written clearly and she had only to read it out. And while she spoke, of her girlhood, her marriage, of the man with the unknown name—his father—of her flight with him, her flight from him, here, to this house, Augustine sat motionless. His eyes considered her, fixed in their contemplation.

She told him of his own coming, of her brother's anger and dismay, of Sir Hugh's magnanimity, and of how he had been born to her, her child, the unfortunate one, whom she had felt unworthy to love as a child should be loved. She told him how her sin had shut him away and made strangeness grow between them.

And when all this was told Amabel put down her hands. His stillness had grown uncanny: he might not have been there; she might have been talking in an empty room. But he was there, sitting opposite her, as she had last seen him, half turned in his seat, fallen together a little as though his breathing were very slight and shallow; and his dilated eyes, strange, deep, fierce, were fixed on her. She shut the sight out with her hands.

She stumbled a little now in speaking on, and spoke more slowly. She knew herself condemned and the rest seemed unnecessary. It only remained to tell him how her mistaken love had also shut him out; to tell, slightly, not touching Lady Elliston's name, of how the mistake had come to pass; to say, finally, on long, failing breaths, that her sin had always been between them but that, until the other day, when he had told her of his ideals, she had not seen how impassable was the division. "And now," she said, and the convulsive trembling shook her as she spoke, "now you must say what you will do. I am a different woman from the mother you have loved and reverenced. You will not care to be with the stranger you must feel me to be. You are free, and you must leave me. Only," she said, but her voice now shook so that she could hardly say the words— "only—I will always be here—loving you, Augustine; loving you and perhaps,—forgive me if I have no right to that, even— hoping;—hoping that some day, in some degree, you may care for me again."

She stopped. She could say no more. And she could only hear her own shuddering breaths.

Then Augustine moved. He pushed back his chair and rose. She waited to hear him leave the room, and leave her, to her doom, in silence.

But he was standing still.

Then he came near to her. And now she waited for the words that would be worse than silence.

But at first there were no words. He had fallen on his knees before her; he had put his arms around her; he was pressing his head against her breast while, trembling as she trembled, he said:— "Mother—Mother—Mother."

All barriers had fallen at the cry. It was the cry of the exile, the banished thing, returning to its home. He pressed against the heart to which she had never herself dared to draw him.

But, incredulous, she parted her hands and looked down at him; and still she did not dare enfold him.

"Augustine—do you understand?—Do you still love me?—"

"Oh Mother," he gasped,—"what have I been to you that you can ask me!"

"You can forgive me?" Amabel said, weeping, and hiding her face against his hair.

They were locked in each other's arms.

And, his head upon her breast, as if it were her own heart that spoke to her, he said:—"I will atone to you.—I will make up to you—for everything.—You shall be glad that I was born."